"Well, hello!"

said a snooty voice from the top shelf. "What've we got here?"

Magnus couldn't see to the top. "Who *are* you?" he asked.

"But *what,* might I ask, are *you*?" A big-whiskered face leaned over the edge and inspected Magnus.

Mice! Magnus bubbled over with happiness. "Oh, merrily munchily mightily mouse, I've found you!"

"Ach! Answer my question," said the mouse.

"I . . . I'm sorry. What did you ask?"

"I asked what are you, wretched white creature!"

Magnus caught his breath. "I'm Magnus . . . and I'm a mouse I am, I am."

Magnus Maybe

ERROL BROOME
Pictures by ANN JAMES

Aladdin Paperbacks

New York   London   Toronto   Sydney   Singapore

This book is a work of fiction. Any references to historical events, real people,
or real locales are used fictitiously. Other names, characters, places, and
incidents are the product of the author's imagination, and any resemblance to
actual events or locales or persons, living or dead, is entirely coincidental.

First Aladdin Paperbacks edition August 2002
Published by arrangement with Allen & Unwin
Originally published in Australia in 1998 by Allen & Unwin

Text copyright © 1998 by Errol Broome
Illustrations copyright © 1998 by Ann James

ALADDIN PAPERBACKS
An imprint of Simon & Schuster
Children's Publishing Division
1230 Avenue of the Americas
New York, NY 10020

Designed by Lisa Vega
The text of this book was set in Simoncini Garamond.

Printed in the United States of America
2 4 6 8 10 9 7 5 3 1

Library of Congress Control Number 2001098776
ISBN 0-7434-3796-9

One

Magnus only wanted to sniff the morning.

The world outside his cage was strange and enormous, and waiting to be explored. He slid down the cardboard tower and across the ice-cream stick drawbridge. The soft wooden wall was nice to nibble.

Nibble and munch. His nose fitted into the hole. He gnawed around the edges until he saw daylight outside the cage. Nibble and gnaw. He flicked his whiskers and slipped through the opening.

So this was the world! If he ran to the edge of the desk, he could see more. If he skiddled down the leg, he could investigate the fringe of the carpet ... the schoolbag ... the shoes by the wardrobe that smelled of boy ... the open doorway ...

When he finally stopped to look around, he knew he was lost. The vinyl was cold and slippery under his feet. He fled across the kitchen and hid behind the refrigerator.

"I don't particulickly like it here," he said. It had been lonely in the cage. But now, wedged in the gloom behind a huge, pulsating monster, he felt more alone than ever before.

His mother had warned that one day he'd be wrenched from his family. She'd seen it happen many times. The warm, safe breeding box would be home for just a few short weeks. As soon as they were old enough, her children were carried off to be sold.

Was it only a week ago that the boy had taken him away?

Magnus remembered how his brothers had begun to bicker in the shop. The black-and-tan one had turned nippy. Yet how he missed them now. All their bites and scratches were nothing compared to this awful loneliness.

Tears glistened on his pink nose. Magnus fluffed himself into a ball and shivered until his eyes could stay open not a second longer.

"That's the end of that," said the boy. "He chewed right through the wall, and now he's disappeared."

"Aren't you going to look for him?" asked the woman.

"Where?" The boy shrugged. "The man in the pet shop told me I'd lose him if he got away. We'll never find him now."

"I don't know why you wanted a mouse in the first

3

place." The woman gave a little shudder.

The boy stiffened his jaw, waiting to feel the loss of his pet. "Will he die, Mum, if we don't find him?"

"I'm afraid anything could happen. He's so young, and he isn't trained to fend for himself."

The mouse castle stood empty on the table. The boy stared at the still-warm bed of wood shavings, the crooked tower and nibbled toys. He shook his head and for a moment his eyes reflected the color of sorrow.

Then his sister called him outside to kick a football.

In the quiet of the night, Magnus woke. He'd missed the meal the boy would have given him, and he was hungry. Sweet warm smells hung over the kitchen. Might there be something for him?

The refrigerator purred. A tap dripped. Magnus crept from behind the fridge and peered around the room. In the dark, he saw everything clearly. He sniffed across the floor, hoping for a crust, a shred of meat, some grains of cereal or vegetable scraps. Any morsel would do. But the kitchen had been swept clean. Every cupboard was tightly shut.

He climbed on the bench and searched for crumbs. Nothing. A drip of tap water was all that soothed his rasping throat.

Magnus dragged his tail in disappointment and looked for a safe spot to hide. Farther on, he found himself treading on carpet. He saw a cupboard set into the wall—and the door open just a slit. He nudged it with his nose and squeezed his body through, to force it open. Standing on his hind legs, he peered into the linen cupboard.

"Well, hello!" said a snooty voice from the top shelf. "What've we got here?"

Magnus couldn't see to the top. "Who *are* you?" he asked.

"But *what*, might I ask, are *you*?" A big-whiskered face leaned over the edge and inspected Magnus.

Mice! Magnus bubbled over with happiness. "Oh, merrily munchily mightily mouse, I've found you!"

"Ach! Answer my question," said the mouse.

"I . . . I'm so sorry. What did you ask?"

"I asked what you are, wretched white creature!"

Magnus caught his breath. "I'm Magnus . . . and I'm a mouse I am, I am."

"Once is enough," said the mouse. "I suppose you

do look a bit like a mouse."

Another nose appeared over the edge of the shelf—and another and another. Five, six, seven pairs of eyes stared down on him.

"I see he *is* some sort of mouse," said the grayest. "Though definitely not one of us."

"A toy," said a posh voice.

"Very washed out," said a scruffy, long-haired mouse.

The row of heads nodded and agreed.

"Where do you belong?" asked the big-whiskered first mouse.

"I . . . in a . . . truly, I don't know." Magnus's heart was beating as fast as a butterfly's wings.

"Don't squeak, boy! Speak up!"

Magnus heard a rustle above, and a gentle voice called, "Don't be so bossy, Mortimer."

"Ach, Martha!" he said. "Leave this to me."

Then her soft eyes looked down at Magnus. "Ah, Mortimer, he's only a child."

Magnus liked her immediately. "How do you do," he said.

"Very well, thank you," said Martha. "It's most comfortable up here on the blankets."

"Are you . . . a family?" asked Magnus.

Martha's nose wobbled with the beginnings of a smile. "Why, yes, we are. A big family." She had the kindest eyes Magnus had ever seen.

"Would I fit in?"

Before Martha could answer, Mortimer directed the others back from the edge and pushed himself forward. "It's almost morning, and there's no room upstairs." He studied Magnus for a moment. "But you could try the bottom shelf."

Magnus breathed out at last, and a quiet warmth spread through his body. "Thank you, Mr. Mortimer," he said, trying not to squeak.

"Get this right," said the big-whiskered mouse. "It's Musculus. Mortimer Musculus."

"Yes, yes I see." Magnus pushed past a plastic cushion and a stack of photograph albums, and curled into a frayed towel stuffed at the back of the cupboard.

He would not be completely alone today.

7

Two

There was hardly a sound from above. In a drowse, Magnus heard muffled voices outside the cupboard. The thunder of footsteps made him hide his head in the towel. Machines squealed and whirred. The man banged a kettle on the bench; the woman burned the toast. Magnus hoped there was some left for him. The boy dropped his books and yelled at the girl, who kept opening and shutting cupboard doors.

Nobody opened the linen cupboard.

When a door banged one last time, the house shifted into a silence so deep that Magnus felt there was nothing else in the world.

"Anyone there?" he called.

"Shh, child," said a voice from above. He thought it was Martha.

Magnus smiled and snuggled deeper into the old, worn towel.

The middle of the day passed, and he knew he had

slept when he heard the rattle of floorboards. Giant footsteps returned and cooking smells slithered through cracks in the door. He couldn't wait for dark.

The Musculus family knew when it was safe to leave their home. "Right!" called Mortimer.

One by one, the mice uncurled and stretched and clambered down the shelves into the room.

Magnus sat and watched as they hurried past. Nobody asked if he'd like to join them. When they had gone, he looked at himself, clean and shining white. Am I so ugly? So washed-out? So different, just a toy? Surely, the man in the shop had said he was a fine mouse. "Take this one," he'd told the boy. "He's got plenty of go in him."

"My go has all went," he said to himself. "I mustn't cry, I'm too big now. I have to look after myself." It was all up to him. He'd find food somehow ... and a family who wanted him.

Before he had time to move, he heard a patter at the door, and a small mouse stood beside him.

Magnus dabbed quickly at a wet patch on his cheek. He felt his ears turn pink.

"Don't you want to come?" said the mouse.

More than anything, he wanted to go. "Did ... did you come back for me?"

The mouse nodded. "I'm Miranda—but hurry, or we won't catch up with them."

Magnus followed Miranda to the kitchen. It looked as clean as ever. She skirted around the edges and pushed him through a crack in the floor. There, under the sink, was the compost bucket.

"We're in luck. The lid's off tonight." She stood back to let him go first. "All the veggies you can eat."

Four or five mice already scrabbled inside the bucket.

"Go on," said Miranda. "Dive in!"

Food at last. And with friends. Magnus leapt into the bucket. "Oh, merrily munchily mightily meal." His tongue tangled on the tastes.

"Take care, child," warned Martha. "There's some moldy bread tonight. We lost Marcus through the mold."

Magnus sneezed, his whiskers coated with crumbs.

Martha laughed and whisked a paw across her nose. "You'll be needing a good cleaning later."

Miranda sneaked up beside him. "Here, we can share this apple core." She turned to a small brown mouse just like herself, only skinnier. "Hurry up, Manuel, you're so slow."

"Leave me alone," said Manuel in a sniffling voice.

"He's such a baby," said Miranda.

The munch and nibble and scuffle of mice was like music to Magnus. He wanted to laugh and sing and shout.

Then Mortimer called them.

"That's our father," said Miranda. "It's time to go outside."

Beside the front door, a small hole led to the verandah. The mice followed Mortimer onto the lawn. Their feet made no sound on the grass.

"Stick together now," said Mortimer. "And eat only as much as you need. Seeds are getting scarce."

The night was eerie. A giant gum tree blocked out the moon and threw deep shadows on the ground. Behind the house, a forest of bracken spread like a black blanket to the horizon. No mouse had ever ventured into the bracken.

Beyond the lavender hedge, a gate opened to paddocks that seemed to stretch forever.

"Is this the end of the world?" Magnus asked Miranda.

"It's just a part of the world," she answered. "It's called Whereabouts. The sign's on the gate." She peered more closely at him. "Don't you like it here?"

"Not particulickly," he said.

He'd never been outside at night before. He'd hardly been outside at all. The cold air stung his skin. His nose felt numb and his ears burned. He jumped when a sharp screech shattered the silence.

Manuel threw himself flat on the grass.

"What's that?" gasped Magnus.

"I'm t-terribly scared of owls," said Manuel.

"What's an owl?"

"A big-eyed b-bird . . . that eats mice. Quick!"

Magnus could see no bird, and the voice without a face turned his stomach to stone. The owl might be anywhere; right here, behind, above, beside him. Magnus couldn't move. He dared not look around.

He wished Manuel would not stick so close. Manuel was following him like a shadow. Magnus didn't have the heart to tell him to keep away; that it wasn't safe near anyone with a white coat. I'm like a light in the dark, he thought. I'll be the first eaten, for sure.

"Everybody inside!" called Mortimer, and the mice poured like a running stream back into the house.

Magnus chased after them. With each step, he imagined the owl clawing at his tail. These fears were all new to him. He'd known nothing like it when he lived in a cage.

Inside the house, Mortimer counted heads. "Seven— and the extra, all safe. Back to the cupboard!"

Magnus returned to his towel on the bottom shelf. So this was what it was like to be free! While he licked his paws and wiped his face and whiskers, he breathed in the comforting mouse smells from upstairs and heard their after-dinner grooming.

Mortimer cleared his throat. "I've got something to say tonight."

It's about me! thought Magnus. He could feel his heart beating. He heard Martha say something in a whisper.

"Ach!" said Mortimer. "Then tell the white thing to come upstairs!"

Martha spoke down through the shelves.

"Magnus, can you come up?"

Can I come up? Just watch me!

Magnus moved so fast that he couldn't remember how he got there.

The Musculus family sat in a half-circle with Mortimer at the head. Some continued to wipe their whiskers and comb their tails with their teeth.

"Sit there," said Mortimer, pointing to a space beside Miranda.

Martha nudged Mortimer. "Introduce everyone."

"Ahem, this is my mate Martha, and over there's Meggsie."

The scruffy one bared his top teeth at Magnus.

"And Madeleine."

The mink-brown mouse preened herself and spoke in her best accent. "How do you do."

"And the youngsters, Manuel and Miranda." He

turned to the old gray mouse who sat apart from the circle. "Tonight Great-uncle Murgatroyd has some words, important words. Murgatroyd is the sage," he explained to Magnus. "He's studied humans, and he knows." He bowed and held out his paw. "Thank you, Murgatroyd."

The old mouse's neck was lost in his hunched, fluffed-out body. His wise eyes settled on Magnus. "Welcome, stranger. What I have to say affects you, too." He wrinkled his nose and nodded slowly. "Hard times are ahead. Of that, I'm certain. The signs of drought are everywhere. Humans are storing hay and ordering extra mulch. They're watching the clouds and muttering in low voices." He paused and nodded. Magnus thought he had gone to sleep.

"So?" said Mortimer.

"Yes." Murgatroyd shook himself. "So there'll be no easy pickings. We all know we can't depend on the compost bucket. From now on we must be diligent and begin to think like humans; save a few grains each night, for the grass may not seed this summer."

He closed his eyes, then opened them to look around the circle. "If we prepare a store of food, we won't starve." He puffed out his chest and dropped his head. Magnus thought he had gone back to sleep, but perhaps he was only thinking.

"Thank you, Murgatroyd," said Mortimer. "Starting tomorrow, everyone will bring back one grain each night for our store."

"Excuse me," said Magnus. "Do you mean me, too?"

Mortimer narrowed his eyes. "It's up to you, if you want to survive."

Survive! "Oh, but I do."

"Then you know how to go about it."

"Wh-what if the owl's there again?" said Manuel.

"Don't be such a wimp," said Miranda. "We'll look after you."

"And now, light's on!" called Mortimer.

Magnus stared.

"He means it's time for sleep," explained Miranda.

"It's almost dawn," said Mortimer, and pointed below. "You can go back down now."

Magnus's lip quivered. "Go, you mean?" The words caught in his throat. "Thank you for having me," he mumbled as he turned to leave.

"Polite chap, isn't he?" said Madeleine, when Magnus had gone. "He must have mixed in good company. I *knew* there was something about that white coat."

Three

The sun battered down by day, parching the paddocks. The grass crackled like dry chips under Magnus's feet.

By night he foraged with the Musculus family and collected seed for the food store. Each night the mice ventured farther, and seed became harder to find.

Every food supply seemed closed to them. The lid of the compost bucket remained clamped shut.

While they searched the scorched ground, Magnus came to know each mouse in the family. Martha was like a calm current in a rough sea, and she cared for him, he was sure. She watched where he trod and coaxed Mortimer to be kind to him.

Madeleine twittered and twitched and pressed Magnus for details of his relatives. "I once knew a mouse called Marmaduke. You don't happen to be connected?"

Magnus opened his mouth to speak, but Madeleine

didn't wait for his reply. "*He* moved in the right circles. It was Marmaduke who gave me a taste for caviar. One rarely sees it these days."

"Pipe down, Mad," said Meggsie. Magnus recognized his scowl and the voice of the one who had called him "washed out" that first night. "Who likes stinking fish?"

Not me, Magnus was going to say. He only needed a simple home and a family who wanted him. He saw Murgatroyd watching with knowing eyes, and felt he could ask his advice if ever he needed it.

After he'd added his grain to the store each night, Magnus returned to his home below. He heard the rustle and scuffle of the family grooming, and listened to their talk.

One night they were talking about him. Meggsie had the loudest voice. "He's not even a proper mouse," he said. "Pale as a ghost. It's like having a spook in the cupboard."

"I *like* the white coat," said Madeleine. "You can tell that boy has breeding."

"A white mouse is bad luck, I reckon," said Meggsie. "Just you wait!"

Magnus wished they wouldn't argue. What am I supposed to do?

Then he heard Martha's voice. "He might be bigger than you, Meggsie, but he's still a child. Give him a chance."

"A chance!" roared Meggsie. "What more does he want? The sooner we kick him out, the better."

"Leave that to me," said Mortimer.

Magnus put his paws over his ears. No, please, no. If only they'd stop.

"Is our young visitor bothering you, Meggsie?" It was Murgatroyd's deep drawl.

"Yes!" Meggsie bellowed. "As a matter of fact, he is bothering me! Did you see him tonight? One lousy grain! A real no-hoper!"

"Well, then . . ." Murgatroyd's voice trailed into thought. "We'll have to find something more important for you to worry about."

I can see trouble ahead, thought Magnus. And all because of me.

Four

If only he could find some extra food. For all of them. Surely, if he set out before the others, he might discover a new supply, somewhere.

The snores and snuffles upstairs told him it was not yet night. No one missed him when he slipped away.

It was risky, he knew, but the humans were less frightening to him than screeching noises in the night.

The man and the woman, the boy and the girl, sat sprawled in big chairs facing in the same direction. All the talk came from a bright square box in a corner of the sitting room. They didn't talk back. Nobody saw Magnus sneak across the carpet and dart up the passage to the front door.

The smell of summer lay across the land. The sun, which had not quite slipped away, cast a pale glimmer on the grass. Magnus sniffed around the rubbish bin, but the lid was tightly closed. Not a scrap spilled to the ground, unless the foxes had beaten him to it. He shivered, and glanced quickly over his shoulder. His eye caught a small flicker of movement.

"Manuel! What are you doing here?"

"I c-came down to talk to you, and you w-weren't there."

"I should have told you not to follow me around."

The small brown mouse hung his head.

"Can't you see it's dangerous!"

"Everything's d-dangerous."

"Oh, all right then. You can help, I suppose."

Together they grabbled among plants in the garden. They nibbled the leathery leaves of geraniums and spat them out in disgust. They ran to the tips of the stems, but the withered flowers held no seeds.

"We must go farther," said Magnus. "Across the paddocks, where we haven't been before."

A kookaburra watched from a tree above and let out a deep-throated laugh. Farther away, a second bird sent a crotchety answer.

"It isn't very f-funny," said Manuel. "C-can we g-go back inside?"

"I don't particulickly like it myself," said Magnus.

Owls and kookaburras! What else might get him? "Let's . . ."

A rush of air and great flapping wings took the words from his mouth. Something sharp stabbed his backside. He leapt sideways. The pointed beak speared into the ground. The kookaburra squawked angrily.

"Run!" screamed Magnus, and tumbled away from the bird.

Manuel stood, as if his legs wouldn't work. Magnus pushed him roughly. "Get going!"

The kookaburra regained its balance and glared as the mice streaked toward the gum tree. It gurgled when its mate swept down to join the hunt. They eyed the two mice, poised for the right moment.

"Here!" gasped Magnus. "Under here, quick!" The tree's gnarled roots spread across the ground, leaving hollows and ruts where the soil had fallen away. "They can't get us here."

They pushed deep into a small cavern, out of reach of prodding beaks. Magnus sank to the ground. "Phew!" His backside was stinging. He'd had a lucky escape.

"Stupid giggler!" muttered Manuel.

"But we beat him—this time."

They huddled in their hiding place and listened to the chorus of birds at nightfall. The kookaburras burbled in knowing voices.

When the singing stopped, Magnus poked his nose from the hole. A flutter in the treetop told him the kookaburras were still there. And in the distance, he saw a small brown shape moving across the yard.

"Miranda!" he yelled. "Stay away!"

She kept coming. Magnus jumped up and down. "Then hurry! Here!"

Miranda stopped and saw him. As she scampered toward the tree the kookaburras swooped. The air whirred above her head.

Then Magnus grabbed her, and they tumbled into the hole together.

Magnus shook himself and stared at Miranda. "What are you doing here?"

"I woke up and Manuel wasn't there. I went

downstairs, and you'd gone too. Did you find anything?"

Magnus pulled a face. "The kookas nearly got us."

"I wanted to tell you something," said Miranda. "Murgatroyd has put Meggsie in charge of the food store."

Magnus wondered why Miranda would come out alone, just to tell him this.

"He said Meggsie needed something big to worry about. The pile must be as tall as a carrot and fat as a pumpkin by the end of summer."

"Sounds a good idea," said Magnus.

"But Meggsie's hopping mad. He's carrying on like a real idiot."

Magnus heaved a sigh. "This is all because of me, isn't it? Murgatroyd gave him the job to keep his mind off me."

Miranda jerked back her head. "How did you know?"

"I heard arguments. I've got good ears. When they kept me in the cage, I listened to humans..."

"They kept you in a cage! How come they didn't kill you?"

"They were nice to me, really. But I *was* a bit frightened at times, especially when the boy picked me up."

"He picked you up! Like a toy?"

Magnus winced. Miranda was no different from all

the others. But he went on. "He had such enormous hands. And when he put me in his pocket..."

"In his pocket!" Miranda's nose twitched and she swayed on her feet. Magnus thought she was going to faint.

"It was nothing, really. I just thought, what if he sits on me? It was rather dark and cramped in there."

She reached over and nuzzled his neck. "I *knew* you were brave."

"Yes, he's brave," said Manuel. "A k-kooka nearly bit his behind."

Me, brave? thought Magnus. "Things just happen to me."

Miranda watched him for a moment before she spoke. "How did you come to get that coat?"

"Like I said, it just happened, and I can't change it. Nothing I eat makes any difference."

Manuel sniffled. "P-please don't talk about food. I'm s-so hungry."

"We're all hungry," Miranda snapped at him. She turned back to Magnus. "One day you'll find something good about your white coat."

Five

Get a tea towel, will you, dear?" said the woman.

The girl opened the door of the linen cupboard. A small, scruffy face looked at her from the middle shelf, then disappeared under a pile of pillowcases.

"Eek!" The girl slammed the door shut.

"Whatever's wrong?" asked the woman.

"A mouse! In the cupboard."

"It's Magnus!" said the boy.

"No, a *real* mouse."

Magnus sat, trembling, on the bottom shelf. What's so wrong with me? he thought. Look at me. I *am* real, I am I am. How could I not be real when I'm shiverivering like this?

"Everybody out!" It was Mortimer. He smacked Meggsie across the nose. "I *told* you to stick to the top shelf. Now we'll have to get out fast, before they come back."

Meggsie pulled a face. "I was only exploring. You

27

gave me this stupid job, and I thought I might find some stray seed around."

"No time for excuses! Get moving!"

The mice spilled from the cupboard, pushing and shoving to be first out of the house. In a corner of the backyard, the woman was hanging washing on the line. They steered away from her, across the garden, past the few straggly fruit trees and the shed with two bicycles leaning against the door.

Behind the shed, they stopped. Mortimer held up a paw. "It's still too light to forage in the open. We must hide away till dark." His eyes scanned the paddock.

"Excuse me," said Magnus. "I know where there's a hollow, big enough for all of us."

Mortimer nodded at him. "Very good, kid. But be quick about it."

Meggsie raced along with Magnus, muttering and grumbling all the way to the gum tree. "Boss of the heap! Hmph! What's the use? Why do I get all the work?"

The family squatted in the earthen cave. "Who'll tell a story to pass the time?" asked Martha.

Nobody answered. Murgatroyd opened one eye and cleared his throat. "Perhaps I could give you a little history."

"I don't want to hear about the past," said Meggsie. "I hate the olden days."

Miranda nudged Magnus. "Tell them about the humans, Magnus."

"Yes, g-go on," said Manuel. "Tell us about people."

"It isn't much," said Magnus. "I was in this cage, and . . ."

"In a cage! A prison?" said Madeleine. "You weren't brought up in a palace or anything?"

"Well, it did have a tower, and things to play with."

"Tell them about the boy," said Miranda.

"The boy looked after me. He fed me every morning and every afternoon."

Madeleine's eyes opened wide. "You mean, he *gave* you food? A servant! You didn't have to find any?"

"There was plenty of food."

"Spoiled brat!" said Meggsie. "I knew you wouldn't know how to find anything."

"It's all right," whispered Miranda. "Go on."

"He used to pick me up and let me run along his arm."

The mice gasped and tittered and shuffled closer to listen.

"It was a rough road, leading up to his shoulder. He

had a huge gaping ear, polished smooth like marble. I peeped inside—ugh!"

"Is this a fact?" asked Mortimer. He twitched his whiskers. "You've been handled by a human?"

Magnus nodded. "When I tickled his ear, he grabbed me by the tail and carried me upside down, back to the cage."

"Ouch!" came a chorus of voices.

"One doesn't want to be treated like something on a string," said Madeleine.

"It didn't hurt," said Magnus. "It was better than being squashed in his fist."

"I've heard," began Murgatroyd, "that people pay to bring mice into their houses. They keep them locked up, as Magnus tells us, and use them as playthings."

"Could we be playthings?" asked Madeleine.

"No way," said Meggsie. "I'd rather starve."

Martha smiled, inviting Magnus to keep talking. "Do you have any other stories?"

"Tell them about the tooth," said Miranda.

"The b-boy didn't *bite* you?" said Manuel.

Magnus laughed. "He couldn't bite anything. His teeth fell out."

"Fell out! A whole tooth?"

"Both his front top teeth, one after the other. He had this big gap. They don't keep growing like ours. New teeth come later."

The mice punched each other and rocked about with laughter.

"They *change* teeth!" said Mortimer. "Is that a fact?"

Magnus nodded. "But only once. After that they get fake teeth. The man had one that he took in and out."

The mice laughed so much, they had to wipe away the tears.

"Their nails keep on growing, but their teeth fall out," said Magnus.

"Peculiar creatures, humans," declared Murgatroyd. "The more we learn about them, the stranger they become."

"And something else," said Magnus. He was beginning to enjoy himself. "They wash *before* eating, instead of after."

"Ach, how disgusting!" said Mortimer. "I always suspected they were dirty things."

"They do smell a bit like a cooked-up compost bucket."

Martha bent toward Manuel. "I hope you're listening, dear. You see how much Magnus knows of the world."

Meggsie grunted and swore under his breath. "Toy boy! Clever little creep, worming his way into our patch like this. But just wait..."

Mortimer coughed and whiskered his way from their hiding place. He sniffed about. "It's safe to move now. The dark has come. We'll need to go far tonight, if we're to find food."

"Rotten drought," muttered Meggsie. "Rotten food store. Don't know why we bother." He jigged on one leg and then the other like a prizefighter. "Some of you are just plain lazy." That was one thing you couldn't say about him. It was hard to catch Meggsie standing still.

He danced toward Magnus and clipped him on the ear. "And you! What use are you?"

Oh, miserable, messy, maddening mouse! thought Magnus. He stared Meggsie in the eye. "One day I'll show you. You'll see!"

Six

The north wind howled across the land and carried the topsoil away with it. Magnus knew he was a failure. Again. He scoured the paddock and couldn't find a single seed.

The mice made their way home with only two grains to add to the pile. They were hungry and weighed down with doubts for the future.

Meggsie vaulted to the top shelf ahead of all the others.

His scream burst like a siren into the night. "Noooo! No! It's gone!"

The family scrambled up to join him. *"Gone!"* they echoed.

The top shelf had been swept clean. There was not a seed left.

Meggsie howled and stamped his feet. "My food store, all gone. How could they do it? Where have they taken it?"

"They've cleaned us out," said Mortimer. "It isn't safe here anymore. We must move house."

"But what about my food store?"

Martha nosed him gently. "Calm down, Meggsie. We have more to worry about at this moment."

"I was looking after it. It was *mine*."

Murgatroyd raised his head and creased his nose in thought. Mortimer looked to him for advice.

"I think . . . ," said Murgatroyd slowly. "I think that from now on we're in grave danger. The humans will be after us. For now, we could move to the toy cupboard. It doesn't get much use these days, and the boy and girl still can't reach the top shelf. We should be safe there."

"It won't be as comfortable," said Madeleine.

"But safer," said Mortimer. "Now let's get going."

Meggsie stared into the corner where the pile had been. "I can't believe it," he mumbled as he trailed the others to the cupboard in the playroom. "All gone. What's the use?"

Instead of blankets and sheets and towels, there were tin drums and building blocks, an old skateboard, and trucks and trains and trumpets. And balls of every size. The mice climbed over them without making a sound. Magnus stopped at the bottom and waited.

"You'd better come up," said Mortimer. "We need to talk." He pushed the toys aside to clear a space for the family. Manuel gave a weak sigh and crouched beside Martha. She stroked his head and smiled across at Magnus. "Come and sit here."

Someone's stomach rumbled. Magnus supposed it was his own.

Mortimer coughed. "Listen to me. We mustn't let tonight's disaster beat us. But from now on, it's red alert. We must stick together. Nobody goes off alone—however hungry."

"What about me, downstairs?" squeaked Magnus.

"Ach! There you are, kid! I'm afraid it's rather cramped up here. You'll be all right down there if you keep yourself hidden."

Magnus had thought they were beginning to like him. He looked up at Mortimer. "Is that all, then?"

Mortimer nodded. "Just don't get discovered. And don't venture out alone."

"Oh!" said Magnus. "I won't. I won't again." He yawned and made his way to the bottom of the toy cupboard. He curled himself into a ball, waiting for the racket and bang of early morning, before the peace of the day descended.

Before long, he heard a rustle and creak from upstairs, and a small figure crept past him.

He lifted his head. "Martha!"

"Quiet!" she whispered. "Don't tell a soul. I have to go. Manuel is faint with hunger. I must find something . . . anything . . ."

"I'll come with you."

"No." Martha held him back. "Stay here and keep guard."

"But it's nearly light."

"I won't be long. There may be something . . . some small thing . . . just a crumb, somewhere in the kitchen."

She slipped through the opening between the doors and disappeared without a sound.

Magnus couldn't sleep, knowing Martha was out there alone. He listened for her return and lost count of the minutes. Surely, the dawn must have come.

He pushed his nose through the door and saw that it was day, though there was no sign yet of the man or the woman, the boy or the girl.

Sunrise cast a honeyed light across the kitchen floor. Magnus stole across the carpet to the brink of the vinyl.

"Martha!"

Martha's contorted body lay on its side. Her head

was jammed under the iron clamp of the trap.

"Martha!" he cried again.

She couldn't reply. Her breath came in gasps. Her eyes followed him and closed as he rubbed his nose against hers. He put his ear to her mouth. "Martha, speak to me."

"Go!" she gasped.

"I won't leave you," he said.

"Go."

The bait that had lured her sat wedged under her nose: a small speck of bacon she'd wanted to take to Manuel. Martha would always have risked her life for her children. Magnus knew that.

"Don't . . . tell . . . anyone," she breathed.

How could he not?

"Just . . . say . . . I . . . I . . ."

Her body shuddered. Blood dribbled from her mouth, but she was still.

Magnus closed his eyes. He lay his head against her breast. "I won't leave you."

Martha. If it hadn't been for Martha, he might not be here today. "Oh, memorable motherly mouse." It was she who had persuaded Mortimer to let him stay. Without her, nothing could be the same. How could he go on? What would he tell the others?

The others! He raised his head and saw the world around him, the kitchen and doors leading to the playroom and the toy cupboard where everyone who loved Martha slept on, not knowing.

He licked Martha's crumpled coat, and his body ached with emptiness. "Forgive me, Martha," he whimpered. "I have to tell the truth."

Then, as he wept there, not wanting to leave her, not wanting to say good-bye, the floor shook under him and the sound of footsteps came closer. Magnus darted behind the sideboard until it was safe to run back to the cupboard.

"Got it! We've got it!" the man shouted.

"Well done, dear."

"Yuk!" cried the girl. "Get it out!"

The boy flipped the trap open and held up the broken body.

"Chuck it in the bin," said the man.

Magnus heard the lid snap shut.

He dragged himself back to the cupboard and lay among the toys, crying out against the day which kept on coming as if nothing had happened.

 *Seven*

"Where's Martha?" Mortimer's question blurted into the early dark of evening.

The mice shuffled about and murmured in low voices.

"I *told* you no one was to go off alone!"

Down below, Magnus shivered. He knew what he had to do. He swallowed and raised his head in the air. "Excuse me . . ."

"Ach, what's that?" said Mortimer.

"It's the spook," said Meggsie.

"Yes," said Magnus. "It's me." He knew they'd be disappointed. They thought, perhaps, it was Martha. "Please?" he called, and his voice hardly carried to the top. "Can I come up? It's important."

"All right," said Mortimer. "What is it now?" Then he saw Magnus's face. "You . . . you know something?"

Magnus looked away. "It's . . ." He didn't know how to tell them. The breath caught in his throat. "I . . . uh . . . uh . . ."

"What've you done now?" cried Meggsie.

Mortimer twisted around and bit him on the neck. "Listen to him, Meggsie!"

"I've . . . I did nothing. I wished I could . . . I wanted to . . ." Magnus sniffed. "But I couldn't."

Mortimer stretched out and touched him. "Sit down, kid. Now tell us."

"I saw Martha go, and I followed her, but it was too late. She's gone."

"Gone? You mean, she's . . . she died?"

Magnus dabbed at his nose. "I'm so sorry."

"How?" Mortimer's voice was steady.

"There was a trap."

"A trap! I knew it! I knew they'd try to get us." Mortimer spoke as if to himself.

Magnus suddenly saw how it all happened. If it hadn't been for him, Meggsie would never have been put in charge of the store. If Meggsie hadn't been in charge of the store, he wouldn't have been caught on the middle shelf that night. If Meggsie hadn't been seen, there would have been no trap. There would have been food in the store, and Martha wouldn't have gone searching for food for Manuel. It's all my fault, just because I'm here. Meggsie was right about me.

"Where did they take her?" Mortimer's voice broke into his thoughts.

"I . . . I don't know." Now he was telling a lie. But he couldn't tell them they'd thrown Martha in the trash bin. Nor would he ever tell them she'd died scrounging food for her child. Little Manuel must never know.

"Tell them . . . tell them . . . ," Martha had said. Tell them what?

Magnus looked from one to the other and said nothing.

"I'd like to know," said Mortimer. "It would help to know."

"I stayed with her," said Magnus. "Till she died. Till they came and took her. I . . . she . . . I can't say."

Mortimer coughed. "It's so hard, just to be told— and nothing. Nothing to grieve over. Just gone!"

Magnus looked up and saw him through a blur.

"I'm sorry, kid. I know you were fond of her too."

Magnus nodded and sniffed, and didn't speak.

"Stay. Stay up here with us. We'll all have to help one another."

Eight

Every day, food became harder to find. And it grew more dangerous to stay in the house.

The woman cleaned out and scrubbed every cupboard, room by room. The man set a trap each night, in a different corner of the kitchen.

Mortimer warned of the hazards and said their days in the toy cupboard were numbered. Hunger might even drive them out before the woman did.

But where to go next?

The family gathered under the clothesline. A string of washing flapped in the warm night wind. "Now, listen here," said Mortimer. "Murgatroyd has decided the toy cupboard's no longer safe. So when we finish foraging tonight, we won't be going back. I know a small space under the floor of the bathroom. It isn't smart, but it should be safe. They'll never think to look for us there."

Madeleine turned up her nose. "Sounds most uncomfortable."

"We only want to survive," said Mortimer.

Manuel whimpered beside Miranda. She reached out and licked his cheek, and they sat in silence.

Murgatroyd lumbered across to Magnus and drew him aside. "You're looking rather miserable, young fellow."

"It's no good," said Magnus. "Everything I touch turns bad. I'm trouble—no use to anyone."

At the front of his mind he could still see Martha's mangled body and the giants that took her away.

Murgatroyd pressed Magnus to the ground. "Listen to me. There'll always be accidents. I've seen so many. What's happened has happened—you must stop mulling over that day. Let it go, and hold on to the good things. That way we'll always have Martha in our lives."

"I'll try," said Magnus.

Murgatroyd patted him on the head. "You've got a better brain than most of us, and you *listen*."

How does he know I listen? thought Magnus. He can't hear me listening. He twitched his nose. If only I wasn't so small. Everything's bigger than me. He'd seen humans from their ankles up, and they towered over him like mountains. It wasn't fair.

"Murgatroyd," he said. "Why are we so small...and they're so enormous?"

Murgatroyd pointed across the paddocks to the distant ranges. The moon shone silver on the peak. "There's a whole world outside Whereabouts, young fellow, and it's bigger than they are." Murgatroyd eased back on his haunches and closed his eyes.

Magnus coughed. "Ahem."

The old mouse flickered his eyelids, as if he listened with his eyes.

"Miranda said this was just part of the world. How much more of the world is there?"

"More than I have time to tell you," said Murgatroyd. "I've heard there are places across the sea, can you imagine? But even in this land there are cities, with hundreds of buildings and thousands of humans. Not so far away, either."

"You mean we could go there? I think, perhaps, I came from the city. I remember some things . . . smells and noises and everything moving."

"Did the boy bring you to Wyetown by train?"

"Train?"

"A vehicle on rails, I've heard, but long and joined in segments like a caterpillar. And like a caterpillar, it twists and turns, but very fast."

"I think it might be a scary thing, a train."

Murgatroyd gazed ahead, as if he were drawing a picture of a train in his mind. "True, young fellow. It won't get out of your way. You don't want to tangle with a train."

Magnus blew out a long, slow breath. Whereabouts seemed a very comfortable place when he thought about it.

He watched, but Murgatroyd had no more advice for him that night. He'd go now and join the others in the search for food. "Hey! Wait for me!" He raced after them.

Meggsie stopped and spun around. He poked his top teeth at Magnus. "I'm not waiting for anyone—especially you!"

Magnus pulled himself up as tall as he could. "I'm coming, anyway. So you'll have to put up with it."

He wondered where his courage had come from.

They tracked over the same ground they had covered the night before and the night before that, as if some miracle might have brought food during the day. The mice were all growing thin. Their bones showed through their coats. Soon Manuel would be too weak to forage with the others.

Magnus decided he had to do something better than this. While the others edged ahead, noses to the ground, he slipped away, back to the house.

Nine

Why hadn't he thought of it before?

He knew the boy kept chocolate in his room. Magnus had watched from the cage while he lay on his bed, listening to his Walkman—and chewing. He always threw the papers on the carpet.

Chocolate wrappers. The smell came back to Magnus now. He ran faster to the boy's bedroom. His heart thumped as he stood in the doorway.

The boy was asleep. Magnus could hear his breathing. In the dark, he saw the bedside table littered with comics. And on the floor, a flake of silver paper. He sniffed the scent of chocolate and licked the paper. It prickled his tongue. If only the boy had spared him a crumb!

He trampled over the paper toward the desk. There, just as he'd left it, stood the cage made to look like a castle. The cardboard tower sagged. The hole, where he'd nibbled his way out, gaped like an open doorway.

It was a door he wouldn't go through again.

The schoolbag lay open beside the chair. A folder and some books spilled to the floor. The bag smelled of stale socks and sandwiches. Magnus dived between the books, down to the dust and grit at the bottom.

He slithered past marbles and pens and rubber bands till he came upon a chocolate bar that was not quite eaten. Hungrily he gulped down the thick, sweet fudge. Then he stopped. He'd come to find food for Manuel!

Caramel oozed down his chin. He wiped it with his paw. There was a mouthful left for Manuel. He dragged the bar from the bag.

With the paper between his teeth, he glanced across to the bed. The boy was watching him! No, it was his imagination. The boy's eyes were shut. His eyelashes fluttered. Magnus couldn't tell whether he was awake or asleep. But he didn't stir.

Magnus pulled the small piece of chocolate in its paper across the bedroom floor, along the passage, and out the front door.

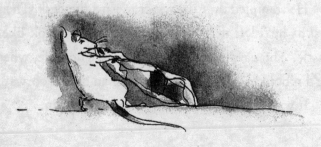

When the Musculus family returned, dejected, from the night's hunt, Magnus was waiting in the yard. He beckoned to Manuel. "Here, this is for you."

"How! Where did you find it?" Manuel grinned, and for a moment Magnus imagined he saw Martha smile too. But it was Miranda who was watching.

"Shh!" he said. "Don't tell anyone, and I can go again."

Mortimer's tired voice directed them under the wall outside the bathroom, and along a pipe to a sheltered spot under the wash basin. "It will have to do," he said. "No complaints."

The boards were dry, though the smell of damp made Manuel cough.

"Squeeze in," said Miranda. "There's room for all of us."

But things were getting worse. The woman was so busy and the house so clean that every tiny pawmark left a telltale sign on the floor. The mice never knew where the next trap might be.

The boy wouldn't miss a leftover chocolate bar, but Magnus couldn't risk taking too much from his room. What if the boy found out? Would he tell on him? Might the parents set a trap inside the schoolbag? Magnus shut his eyes. It was too frightening to think about.

Ten

Day after day, the paddocks shimmered and whined under a hard-hearted sun. Even the moon shone bloodred over the land.

The mice slept uncomfortably in their cramped, wooden quarters under the wash basin. Hunger and lack of sleep made them irritable. They snapped at one another.

Magnus fitted in the best way he could, without losing his temper. Slowly the sight of Martha's wracked body faded from his mind, and he saw her again as he'd known her, small and bustling and gentle. He could even smile now when he thought of her.

But it hurt him to see Miranda. She followed him with sad eyes and never spoke of her mother. Before, she'd led the way. "Let's do this." And, "Come and see that." Now she walked behind him, scarcely looking where she was going.

One dark morning, she settled under a shrub beside

him. Magnus leaned close and spoke
softly. "I feel right about Martha
now," he said. "I want you to feel
that way too."

She gazed at him, not
believing he could say anything to help her.

"I've stopped feeling sad, because of all the things I
want to remember. The gap has filled up with good
memories," he said, and realized he was talking like a
grown-up. "It's what you carry with you that counts."

Miranda was silent for some time, and then she said,
"Thank you."

Magnus felt warm inside, till Meggsie bounced up
and cuffed him under the chin.

"Buck up, kid!"

"I *am* bucked up," said Magnus. Why couldn't
Meggsie leave him alone?

"Typical teenager!" said Madeleine, suddenly.
"Thinks he knows everything!" She spoke so Meggsie
could hear. "Don't let it worry you, Magnus."

Meggsie glared at her, but it didn't stop her from
talking. "He's jealous, that's all. He didn't grow up in a
palace like you."

"But . . . ," said Magnus. "But I didn't . . ."

"I know you didn't want to talk about it. But you can't help what you are."

Magnus gave up. "That's true."

Meggsie mimicked Madeleine's voice. "Poor little fellow, you can't help what you are. . . ."

"Oh, pipe down!" said Magnus.

Meggsie spun around. "So! The wimp's got some spunk in him!"

"Control yourself, Meggsie," called Mortimer. "We have enough problems as it is."

"Yeah!" Meggsie bared his teeth at Magnus. "And who's making it worse, eh?"

"Not M-M-Magnus!" Manuel stood and faced Meggsie.

Meggsie swiped at his cheek and knocked Manuel to the ground.

Magnus leapt up, with his paws in the air. "Hit *me*, you bully! Now who's a wimp?"

Meggsie tossed back his head and jigged and dodged, taunting him.

Magnus jumped on him and knocked Meggsie down. He pressed his paws into Meggsie's neck.

Meggsie bit and kicked as they wrestled on the ground.

The young mice stood and cheered.

"Cease!" called Mortimer. "We'll all be discovered."

Magnus pushed Meggsie away. Meggsie glared. His cheeks twitched, as if the blood were boiling under his skin. Then he let out his siren scream and belted into Magnus with both front paws. Head down, he butted Magnus in the chest.

Each time Magnus pushed him off, Meggsie came again. Magnus roared and threw his full weight at Meggsie. He belted the left jaw, the right jaw, and then the left again. Meggsie's head jerked back, and his legs crumbled under him.

Magnus stood over him for a moment, then walked away.

The mice fell silent, staring at Meggsie on the ground.

Then Madeleine ran after Magnus. "Come back! Meggsie started it!"

Meggsie sat up slowly, not looking at anyone. When he dragged himself to his feet, he sidled past Magnus with his face turned away.

"Let him go!" said Mortimer. "He'll be back."

Magnus felt bruises coming already. He sat down wearily and licked the scratches.

"You did well," said Madeleine. She preened herself. "Do you think, one day, you could introduce me to your family?"

Ever since he was little, Magnus had blushed at difficult moments. If anyone talked about him, or asked tricky questions, he felt his ears go red. Like now. "I . . . I don't think I could find them." The truth was, he'd grown away from his family. This was his home now— or he wanted it to be. Yet even Madeleine, who was his friend, still thought of him as different.

"One must miss them, surely," she said.

Magnus shook himself. "Miss them . . . who?"

"Your family."

"Oh!" He didn't want to disappoint her. "They . . . we were brought up to go our own ways."

56

"Adventurers, of course!"

This was true, too. He *was* having adventures, even if he didn't seek them. "Yes," he said. It was good not to have to tell a lie.

"I'm so glad you came."

Magnus caught sight of Miranda, and she winked at him. He was surprised just how good a wink could make him feel.

When Madeleine sauntered back toward the house, he and Miranda rolled on the ground and giggled till their eyes were full of tears.

"What am I going to do?" gasped Magnus. "She still thinks I grew up in a palace. She won't believe anything else."

"She wants to believe it," said Miranda. "She's such a dreamer."

Magnus grunted. "So I end up telling fibs. It's all so stupid."

"But don't spoil the story now. Can you imagine how she'd like to hear you say this? 'I was born in a cage, and sent to a pet shop . . .'"

"which smelled like a stable . . ."

"where I was sold to a boy . . ."

"and came to Whereabouts in a shoebox!" Magnus

grinned at her. "It does spoil the story a bit."

"So let her believe in the palace."

"In time I might come to believe it myself." He flicked his pale whiskers. "I could even begin to think I'm important."

"But you are," she said shyly.

Eleven

Clouds massed on the horizon and vanished as if the sun had sucked them dry. Dust coated the leaves of trees, and parrots fell dead from the branches.

The mice held meetings, but they couldn't change the world. Meggsie was strangely silent, and in their dingy bathroom they were all too dejected to argue.

Mortimer issued an order. "I've checked out the house, and it's a minefield. This is war! No room, no cupboard is safe. Nobody is to go inside that house again!"

Magnus glanced across at Manuel. He had to go, in spite of Mortimer's rule.

That night, while the others foraged on the barren earth, Magnus crept back into the house. He saw the first trap beside the back door. How he wanted the speck of bacon that tempted him!

He trod warily, sniffing for warning smells. The second trap lay near the entrance to the living room. He held his breath, so he couldn't smell the bacon as he passed.

The boy's breathing was slow and even, and Magnus knew he was asleep. He climbed first on to the bedside table, but there was not a trace of food. He wondered why he felt such disappointment, as if somehow he'd expected the boy to leave something there.

Magnus crept closer and gazed at the boy, as though being asleep made him less real. His hair was dark on the pillow. Magnus stretched his neck till his nose almost

touched the boy's cheek. His skin smelled warm and salty. Magnus pulled back. His eyes traced the outline of the body under the cover. Beside him on the sheet lay a shape like a butterfly net.

Magnus reminded himself that he'd come for food. The table rattled as he tumbled down the leg, but the boy slept on. Magnus scurried across the floor to the schoolbag. It was a lucky dip. Anything could be inside that bag.

He pushed past the folder and slipped underneath the pencil box. *Splitt!* A pencil rolled out. He ran down the ruler to the bottom of the bag. There it was! He smelled it before he saw it, a peanut chocolate bar, only half finished. It wasn't like the boy to leave so much uneaten.

Magnus nibbled on the crunchy part. The paper rustled in his ear. He tried not to gobble, or it would all be gone. Only one bite more of peanut, and a mouthful of the chocolatey part. But if he bit off just one more piece of nut, the bar would be easier to carry away.

There, he'd left enough for Manuel to feed on. He dragged the remains of the bar out of the bag and across the floor. The sheet swished on the bed, and the boy rolled over. Magnus stopped, as if he'd been pierced by an arrow. He glanced up, without moving, without even raising his head.

The boy pushed back the sheet and sat up.

Magnus held his breath. He tried to run away, but he couldn't move. His legs were numb, like dead limbs under him.

He dropped the chocolate bar, *plip!* to the carpet. His heart thudded in his ears, but his body felt like a hollow stem, empty inside. I still have my head, he thought, but I can't think what to do. Was this the end for him? Had he betrayed the others?

The boy leaned over and switched on the bedside lamp.

Magnus was captured in the sudden blinding light. He stared at the floor, all feeling gone. The room was a prison, with nowhere to hide.

The boy reached for the butterfly net. With his fingers around the handle, he pulled himself up slowly and sat, staring at the mouse. His eyes hardly blinked.

He swung his legs over the side of the bed.

I'm done for! thought Magnus.

The boy's hand tightened around the net. He leaned down and gazed at the small figure on the carpet. Then he dropped the net back on the sheet.

Magnus knew this was his chance to run. But something kept him there. He dared now to lift his head and look at the boy.

The boy reached out and grasped Magnus by the tail. He pulled him up, level with his face. Magnus dangled there, and for a moment the boy's eyes met his own.

"Hello, Magnus," he whispered. Then, gently, he placed the mouse back on the carpet.

"Is anything wrong?" called a voice from another room.

The boy switched off the light. "No, Mum, it's nothing." He smiled and lay back against the pillow.

Magnus picked up the chocolate bar and bolted out of the house.

 Twelve

Where did you get it?" asked Miranda.

Manuel passed her a small piece of chocolate, because there was more than enough for him.

"It's a secret," said Magnus.

"That's not fair," said Miranda.

"I can't go back there. We'll have to think of something else."

"It's hopeless," said Miranda. "We've been everywhere."

"Have you been to the top of those mountains?" Magnus looked to the ranges that Murgatroyd had pointed out to him.

"We can't go there."

"Why not?"

"It's too far."

"Not if we find food, it isn't. We could all move there."

Miranda gaped at him. "You mean, leave Whereabouts? But we've always been here."

"We might find a new home, better than this," said

Magnus. "Someone's got to go. Do you want to try?"

"C-could I come?" asked Manuel.

Magnus gave him an understanding lick. "Maybe, later on."

"All right, I'll come," said Miranda.

By now everybody was listening. "When will you set out?" asked Mortimer.

"Tomorrow, very early," said Magnus. He turned to Manuel. "We'll try to bring you back something."

"Something classy?" said Madeleine. She ran a paw down her body.

"To eat, silly," said Miranda.

Meggsie grunted. "You won't get me burning my feet on those hills."

"One always knew Magnus was an adventurer," said Madeleine.

Magnus wished she wouldn't make so much fuss. He was relieved when they could get going. They set out well before daybreak and soon reached the next small farm, where a dog slept chained inside an empty oil drum.

Cows lay like dark shapes against the skyline. In the silence, Magnus could hear their jaws shifting from side to side. He heard the crackle of his own feet on the grass, and Miranda's beside him. And then, the same crackle, fainter, as if they'd left behind an echo of their footprints. Or someone else was there.

Stars lit a path across the valley. They passed the place with the donkey and the old rotting tractor in the yard, and came close to the chicken man's property. Hens were scruffing out of their sleep. A rooster bellowed to welcome the dawn.

Magnus jumped.

"Haven't you heard a rooster before?" said Miranda.

He shrugged. "I don't par . . . particularly like it. But I *have* heard of roosters. My mother told me about a lot of things."

The house at the end of the row of small farms stood in darkness. "That's where the old boy lives," said Miranda. "The one who feeds the birds."

"Birds? Why doesn't he feed us?"

"He thinks we're pests."

"Pests! Like grubs and snails, you mean?"

Miranda giggled. "Silly, isn't it!"

The ground bristled, and the shed's tin roof cracked with the changes in the air.

"I wish I didn't think someone was following us," said Magnus.

"There are always strange noises in the night," said

Miranda. "But we must watch out for snakes."

Magnus shuddered. "A snake . . . I couldn't handle."

"They can eat a mouse—a possum, even—in one go."

"Don't tell me now."

The small clump of shops and a train station called Wyetown slept on. Magnus and Miranda hurried past, into open country. The sun's first rays fingered the tree trunks and lightened the sky. The earth stretched as far as they could see, threadbare, like an old, rubbed, gray blanket.

"There's not enough food here for even the smallest insect," said Magnus. "We might find something higher up."

He kept his eyes on the tallest peak. Higher still, he saw a dark dot in the sky. As it grew bigger and the thrum of its body swelled to a roar, he ducked his head and flung himself to the ground. Owls and kookaburras—and now this! "A mechanical bird!"

Miranda laughed. "An aircraft, you mean. It's harmless. We get them overhead sometimes, but they keep their distance."

"Phew!" Magnus dusted himself and hoped she wouldn't think he was just a kid. "Of course," he said. He watched the aircraft shrinking back to a dot. "Let's keep going."

The burning soil blistered their feet. They darted from bush to bush, desperate for a few seconds of shade. Plants that lay ahead turned out to be dry sticks. But then Magnus found a thistle, a single thistle alive among the skeletons of dead plants.

They pounced on the prickly stalk and nipped it off at the ground. Magnus dragged it under the shelter of a hollowed root, and together they picked at the seed heads. "One for you . . . and one for me."

They nibbled, but not much, while the afternoon simmered outside. It was a good place to rest till the pain had gone out of the day.

"I never thought I'd be in places like this," said Magnus.

"But you've been everywhere," said Miranda. "You said the shop smelled like a stable. When were you in a stable?"

"Not me, my mother. Once, she lived in a stable, and in the shop it all came back to her. She told us about the cushion of straw, and sweet, warm smells, and chaff and oats—plenty for everyone."

"I can see it," said Miranda.

Magnus edged closer, till he could feel Miranda's soft coat brushing against his own.

"Do you think some things are *meant* to happen?"

"Oh, no," she said. "Things just happen."

He was quiet.

"What's wrong?"

"I used to think that. Things just happened to me. And I couldn't make anything different. But lately I've been thinking, maybe . . . just maybe I *did* make something happen."

"Like what?"

"Like going out to explore that morning. I only wanted to look around. I thought I was lost . . . but I found you."

"Oh!"

He noticed her ears turning pink.

"And now . . . we're going out exploring together, and who knows what we'll find!"

She smiled at him. "I never thought like that before."

"Maybe things can happen when you start something. And then you find something you never expected. In a way, maybe Madeleine was right. I *am* an adventurer."

"Then what do you think we'll find?" she asked, and nestled against him.

His mind was filled with flickering lights, and he didn't know whether to listen to his head or his heart. "Um . . . um . . . ," was all he could say.

Thirteen

When the sun slipped behind the ranges, Magnus and Miranda ventured from their shelter and began the trek to the summit.

"I'm hungry again," she said.

"Me too."

"The grass is worn away right to the top of the hill."

"Don't give up yet."

There was not a blade of grass in sight. Above, the ground became rocky. They puffed as they climbed higher.

Two black specks circled above the summit, keeping watch on the world below.

"Eagles!" said Miranda.

"There's always something," said Magnus. They'd need to keep well hidden from now on.

The air hissed and blew dust in their faces. But it wasn't just the air. Suddenly the soil swished ahead of them, and Miranda stood still. She saw the shiny black rope looping around the rocks. "Snake!"

"It's coming!" cried Magnus. He grabbed her tail in his teeth and tried to pull her back.

The snake's forked tongue flicked in and out as it wound toward them. Its eyes glinted.

Magnus looked up. There was only one chance. "The tree! Make for the tree!"

They darted over stones and scrambled up the trunk. In one quick lunge, the snake was at the base of the tree.

"Go higher!" yelled Magnus. "Can it climb?"

"It isn't a tree snake," said Miranda. She grappled for a hold on the bark.

"Hang on!"

The snake coiled around the trunk and hovered with its head in the air. Its tongue flickered furiously.

"It's hungry!" said Miranda.

"Higher! Climb higher!" They were only a dog's leap off the ground.

"I can't."

The bark crumbled under their claws.

"The tree's dead," said Magnus. "It's all falling apart."

They clung there, not halfway up the trunk, unable to reach the branches.

"I'm scared," said Miranda.

Magnus was too afraid to breathe. He was losing his

grip on the tree. Splinters of bark fell about him.

A shadow passed over the ground, but there was no sound. Then, in a rush of air, an eagle swished down and scooped the snake from the tree. Without pausing, it rose back into the sky with the snake dangling from its beak.

Magnus breathed out. He tumbled down in a hail of bark. Miranda scrambled after him. They lay there trembling, and watched as the two eagles disappeared into the distance.

"Phew!" Magnus shook the grit from his body and stood up, testing his legs. "Who would have thought we'd be saved by an eagle!"

"I couldn't have held on another second," said Miranda.

"Let's get out of here."

They stumbled uphill, over crags and ruts and furrows. Each hump they overcame led on to another. But then, ahead, they saw a single boulder, smooth and round, standing against the sky. They had reached the top.

"We're here!" sang Magnus, and wheeled around to feel the air on every side.

Miranda held her breath. "It's . . . wow!"

Under a purpling sky, the world sprawled below as if someone had made patterns on paper. Pocket handkerchief paddocks lay between dark lines of trees. A riverbed wound mud brown through the flats.

"Don't you feel small up here!" she said.

"Not a bit. Look down! See those splodges of red roofs ... see those dots, those tiny things moving about like ants?"

"Yes." She squinted into the distance.

"They're people! Humans! Now see how big we

are!" He pulled himself up tall and nuzzled her cheek.

She laughed. And as they stood on the mountain top, it seemed nothing was beyond their reach.

Going home was easier.

They'd found no food, yet their weary bodies carried them along breezily, as if they were only at the start of their journey. They were empty-handed, but their heads were full of discoveries.

In the cool of night they traveled, and reached the edge of the small farms at daybreak. There, Magnus stopped. "We've got nothing to take back to Manuel. What are we going to say?" Then he remembered the old boy who fed the birds. "Seed! He must give them wild birdseed."

She nodded. "We've been out there, in his yard, and all we got were husks."

"But where does he keep it?"

Miranda looked blankly at him.

"You mean, nobody's ever tried to find out?"

"It's a long way to go for nothing."

"Not when we're desperate!" He grinned and

danced in a circle on the dusty road. "Miranda, we might have found a new supply of food after all!"

Miranda sniffed the air. "Shh! Did you hear something? Someone's coming."

They darted behind a fencepost. Nothing moved. The place was silent. Only a twig cracked on the ground across the road.

"I'm sure I heard something, quite close," she breathed.

"It's nothing."

Then a light flicked on in the house and a door opened. The old boy stumped toward the shed.

"We can't go to the shed now," whispered Magnus. "But we can come back tonight. We can promise Manuel a surprise."

The others clambered about Magnus and Miranda when they climbed into the bathroom that morning.

"What did you get?"

"Did you find food?"

"Tell us! Show us!"

Magnus and Miranda felt suddenly weary. They had failed.

"Nothing?" said Mortimer.

"Nothing." Magnus could hardly mouth the word.

"Nothing," said Miranda. Her eyes were beginning to close.

"But we have another idea," said Magnus. "Tonight I'll tell you." He looked around. "Where's Meggsie?"

"I *knew* he'd be late home this morning," said Mortimer. "He went off on his own again. But you can't tell Meggsie anything."

Murgatroyd grunted. "The day Meggsie asks for advice, we'll know he's grown up."

He won't be asking me, thought Magnus, as he snuggled against the bare boards. Home had never seemed so peaceful.

Fourteen

Late in the day, Meggsie staggered into the bathroom.

"Wake up! Look at this! I did it!" He dumped a load of seed in the middle of the sleeping mice. "I've found a new food store for all of us."

Magnus heard a murmur of excitement, or was it his stomach rumbling again?

"Food!" The mice cheered.

Mortimer roused himself, coughed, and slapped his tail across Meggsie's back. "Well done, Meggsie. Where did you find it?"

Meggsie puffed out his chest. "I got to thinking. That old boy who feeds the birds, he must keep the seed somewhere. So I went and looked for it—and I found it in the shed. A whole new sack! Sometimes you just need to use your head."

Miranda widened her eyes at Magnus. He leaned across and whispered, "You were right! There *was* someone there this morning."

"That's Meggsie all right! Snooping around again!" But she smiled at Manuel. "There you go, Manny. A surprise!"

"This is a good day for all of us," said Mortimer. "Thanks to Meggsie, we know where to go tonight. It's farther than usual, and we must be careful not to take too much. Just a little each night, so the old boy doesn't notice the sack going down."

"He won't notice," said Meggsie. "I gnawed through the bottom of the sack, so it spilled out on the floor. Quick and easy—and he won't catch us inside the sack."

"*T-t-t.*" Murgatroyd clicked his tongue, with his head still sunk on his chest. "The old boy will know a mouse has been at his sack."

"But he didn't see me!"

"You left your mark, as surely as if he'd seen you. Never, *never* bite through the bottom. It's a dead giveaway."

Meggsie stamped his foot. "Ungrateful! That's what you are!"

Magnus thought Meggsie was going to cry.

"No matter what I do, it isn't right!"

"Calm down, Meggsie," said Mortimer. "Let's eat and be thankful. And perhaps all is not lost. We must wait for tonight to find out."

The mice moved together by night, across the paddocks and past the small farms toward the old boy's shed.

The sinking feeling in Magnus's stomach gave him more pain than his feet, which still ached from the journey. "I don't know why we're bothering," he told Miranda.

"It's worth a try," she said. "But I'm just *so* mad at Meggsie."

"Don't let Meggsie worry you. If the seed's there, that's all that matters."

"I'm still mad at him. It was *your* idea, and he pinched it. Now it's Meggsie's idea."

When they reached the old boy's property, Mortimer called them to stop. "All right, Meggsie, you go in and see if the shed's safe for us."

In less than a minute, he was back. He flopped on the ground without saying a word.

"Well?" said Mortimer.

Meggsie shook his head. "Nothing!"

"I knew it," said Miranda. "He's messed it up."

"Not a grain of seed," said Meggsie. He lay on the ground, moaning.

"D'you think we could find it if we searched?" asked Mortimer.

Meggsie pounded the earth, as his disappointment turned to rage. "The stingy old boy! He's tipped it all into a bin—with a tight lid. I tried and I tried, but I couldn't open it. None of us would budge it."

Mortimer nodded as if he'd known it would turn out this way, but he said nothing.

Madeleine glared at Meggsie. "One would think you could sometimes use your brains."

"Leave him alone!" Mortimer frowned at her. "He's more upset than any of us."

Meggsie couldn't do a thing right. Magnus knew the feeling. He moved to speak to him, but Meggsie buried his face in the ground.

Mortimer gestured to Magnus to sit down. "Rest a while," he said, "and then we'll head back. But while we're here, we'd better start thinking."

"I'm s-so hungry," said Manuel.

"Shoosh," said Miranda. "We're all hungry."

"One is almost ready to give up," said Madeleine.

"Never!" Mortimer pointed at her. "Never say that again."

Then Magnus had an idea. "Do you think, maybe, we could find our way to the city?"

"Ach, it's such an expedition for all of us."

"The streets, I think, would be overflowing with food. And there'd be places where we could make a home."

"We might never be hungry again," said Miranda.

"Wh-what about all those humans?" said Manuel. "They're s-so enormous."

"Not so enormous," said Magnus. "Sometimes they can seem quite small."

Meggsie lay with his eyes shut and his hair over his ears, but Magnus knew he was listening.

"What do you think, Meggsie?" asked Mortimer.

Meggsie pulled a face. "I think this place stinks. So I suppose the city couldn't be worse."

"Then perhaps I could have a volunteer scout, to go off and investigate?" said Mortimer.

The mice murmured among themselves.

"Maybe Magnus," said Mortimer. "How about it, Magnus, seeing it was your suggestion?"

Meggsie lifted his head. "Magnus? You've got to be joking!"

"Good choice!" said Madeleine. "Magnus knows the ways of the city."

The ways of the city! Magnus shuddered. He didn't even know the way *to* the city. "Oh, mistakenly muddled mouse!" he murmured to Madeleine. "Truly, I don't."

"And how will you travel?" asked Mortimer.

"How will I get there?" Magnus fidgeted with the doubts in his head. "Murgatroyd has told me about trains. I could get the train from Wyetown to the city."

"A free ride!" said Meggsie.

"I think, perhaps, you should not go alone," said Mortimer.

Magnus looked around the circle. Not Mortimer, not Manuel, not Madeleine, not Miranda this time. Magnus knew who it should be. "Would Meggsie like to come?"

Meggsie lifted his head and stared at Magnus. His mouth hung open. "Me?" he croaked. "You mean me?"

Miranda gasped. "Meggsie! Why not me?"

"Meggsie needs it," he whispered. "We'll get on all right together. And I'll find us a house."

She turned her head away and could say no more.

Meggsie stood up and brushed the hair from his face. "Okay, I'll go. I reckon I could show you a thing or two."

Magnus wondered what he'd let himself in for.

Fifteen

By night the family gathered to say good-bye.

Miranda had not spoken to Magnus since the day before. Now she hid behind Mortimer and stared at the ground.

Magnus rubbed noses with Mortimer and Murgatroyd, and gave Manuel a parting nip on the neck. Madeleine stepped up to Magnus and rubbed her nose on his. She nodded to Meggsie. "Good luck, fellows, we'll miss you."

"We're off, then." Meggsie jogged on the spot, anxious to get going.

At last Magnus came to Miranda. He didn't know when he'd see her again. "Miranda?" he said.

She hung back and wouldn't look at him.

"Good-bye, then," he said, and turned to go. "Right, Meggsie?"

Meggsie was already on his way. Magnus followed, dragging his feet in the dust. Each step was taking him farther away. Would he ever see her again?

As they neared the gate he turned to look back. The others waved, but Miranda stomped off in the opposite direction.

"She looks really mad," said Meggsie.

"Where's she going?"

"Who knows? Come along." Meggsie dragged him on.

Magnus was afraid of what might happen to her.

"She's old enough to look after herself," said Meggsie.

"I'm not sure," murmured Magnus. He wasn't sure of anything right now. He took one last look as Miranda disappeared behind the house.

Meggsie started out at a hare's pace and kept ahead of Magnus all the way. "You're lagging," he said.

Magnus knew it. "I can't help wondering," he said. "Where do you think she was going?"

"Who?"

"Miranda, of course."

"Oh, her," said Meggsie. "Nowhere, I bet. She'll calm down and be back with the others by now."

"I suppose so," said Magnus. But he wasn't so sure.

When they came to Wyetown, they stopped beside a

clump of rocks near the train station. "Do you really mean to catch a train?" said Meggsie.

"It'll get us there in a couple of hours."

"But it'll be daylight. What if we're seen?"

"Are you afraid?"

"Of course not!" snorted Meggsie.

"Good. Then we'll wait here till the train comes."

"Boring!" Meggsie shuffled from one foot to another. "What are we going to do?"

"We can talk," said Magnus.

"Talk!" Meggsie caught his breath. "No one wants to talk to me."

"That's not true."

"It *is* true. But you wouldn't notice. You don't notice anything."

"I do! I'm a good noticer. I've noticed lots of things about you."

"Is that why you don't like me?"

"I never said I didn't like you."

"But you don't," said Meggsie. "I can tell. Nobody likes me."

"Rubbish!" Magnus leaned closer to Meggsie. "You see, I've had this feeling all along, there's something the same about you and me."

"You mean, no one likes you either?"

Magnus coughed. "For a while no one seemed to want me. And everything I did went bad."

Meggsie sat down and curled his tail around his body. "Me too. I've tried, ever since Marcus died . . . but you never knew about that."

"Martha told me—he died of the mold."

Meggsie gaped at Magnus. "Did she tell you that? What else did she say?"

"I don't know any more."

"Marcus was never very strong. He was always last to the food. So one night, I found a crust and I carried it home to him. I didn't know the green stuff was mold. They said I knew, but I didn't. I only wanted him to have some bread."

"It was just bad luck," said Magnus.

"They blamed me when he got sick. They've always blamed me."

"I think you've got it wrong. *You* blame yourself."

Meggsie sniffed. "Nothing I ever do makes things better."

Magnus couldn't say any more. He was beginning to sound like Murgatroyd, and he didn't want to become a sage. He wanted to be a friend.

Neither of them had seen dawn seep through the darkness, bringing with it another yellow day. The station stood bathed in early sunlight. A car pulled up on the gravel and a man in a suit leaped out, slammed the door, and ran to the platform. Another car parked alongside, and two women hurried after him.

"Listen!" said Meggsie. In the stillness, faraway, came the faint *t-toodle-oo t-toodle-oo* of an engine. "Is that the train coming?"

"Wait." Magnus held him back. "We'll slip on at the end, so we're not seen."

The people were so intent on boarding the train and finding a good seat that they didn't notice two mice at their heels.

"Mind the step," said Meggsie.

It was quite a jump, and they made it just in time. They fell to the floor as the doors slid shut behind them.

"Over there." Meggsie pointed to spare seats near the back of the carriage.

"Sorry," said Magnus. "Under here. We can't risk being seen, especially me. Don't forget I'm white."

Meggsie snorted at him. "As if you need to tell me."

They hunched in a corner under a seat as the train gathered speed. Miles of scorched paddocks flicked past the window. But all they saw were legs and shoes and sandals.

Now and then the train stopped, and more people filed into the compartment. At a stop called Midland a man in uniform entered the carriage. Two black shoes passed down the aisle. "Tickets, please!"

The mice pressed close together as the shoes stopped just a whisker from their hiding place.

"Phew! That was close," breathed Meggsie when the man moved on.

"Where do you think we are?"

"Under the seat, that's all I know."

"Where do you think *she* is?"

"Who?"

"Miranda, of course."

"Oh, her." Meggsie grunted. "Can't you stop thinking about her?"

"I *am* a bit worried." She could walk into the path of a snake. She wasn't looking where she was going. He saw again the snake's forked tongue and a jaw that stretched like elastic to slip around rats and mice—mice like Miranda, running away from home.

Magnus shook himself. He didn't really know she was running away. Then where was she going?

It was his fault. She was mad at him. He could have told her that all he truly wanted was to have her with him. He thought she knew. Things were working out with Meggsie, too. Why didn't she understand? She could have tried. He felt a sudden surge of anger toward Miranda before he stopped and thought: this is not the way I want to feel.

Sixteen

While the train sped toward the city, Miranda strode on, through the sun-streaked stubble toward the darkening bracken.

Her rage had changed to quiet determination. She would keep going. Now she could think of what to do. Things Magnus had said stuck in her mind: the smell of the stable, the comfort of the stall. She would find that stable. Well, not exactly *that* stable, but one like it.

She'd heard talk of a pony club across the valley. And where there were ponies there must be stables. To get there she would have to go through the great barrier of bracken that had never been crossed.

No mouse would set foot in the forbidden forest. There were stories of giant mouse-eating spiders, and a black feral cat that hunted in the bracken. But she would do it. She'd show the family they could all do it.

She pushed on, down, down into the depths of the gully. The shade enclosed her like a warm tent, locking her in with all the wildlife of the forest floor. Fallen ferns pricked her stomach. The dry leaves were alive with the rustle of insects and small birds.

Miranda tried not to think of what else might be around. But with every step she saw in her mind the wild cat, yellow-eyed and tiger-striped from the sun flickering through the bracken stalks.

If I disappear, I won't be here—and I won't be there. Just *missing*, which means I'm not anywhere.

She pressed ahead, too far into the forest now to turn back.

On the train went, stopping more often now. Dusty shoes crammed the aisle. Briefcases and bags squashed the mice into a corner.

They didn't know how long they'd been hidden away before the train slowed and all the feet turned toward the door. When the doors opened, the shoes shuffled, heel to toe, down to Platform 8.

After the last passenger left and the train was empty, Magnus and Meggsie moved from under the seat and stared out the door. "It's the rest of the world!" cried Magnus.

Platform after platform lay spread before them. Beyond the great station, tall buildings crowded the sky.

"Blocks from the toy cupboard!" said Meggsie. "Only these have grown up."

They jumped to the platform and scampered under a bench as legs and feet pounded past them.

"Listen!" said Magnus.

"What can we hear?"

"It isn't any noise I know. It goes on and on, but I can't hear what it's saying."

Meggsie turned his head to one side. "It's the way the city talks—or kind of hums."

They crouched under the bench while people hurried this way and that and bumped into one another. Trains rumbled in and out of the station. Horns blared and sirens sounded as the city went on humming.

Magnus and Meggsie watched and listened, and decided to sleep—if they could—till the bustle of the day was over. Between the bench and a pillar, a deep crevice hid them from view. They crammed together, and waited.

When the sun had gone down, and lights were switched on all over the city, Meggsie nudged Magnus. "I'm so stiff, I can hardly move."

"Are you ready to go, then?"

Meggsie stretched and nodded. "City, here we come!"

Seventeen

When they became used to the noise, they noticed the smells. The fumes and smoke and cooking smells made them cough.

"How do humans breathe?" asked Meggsie.

"Through very big noses," said Magnus.

Even at night, the streets were full of people. But there was food, too. Food like they had never seen before. Garbage bins lined the alleys, and warm, oily smells filtered through ducts in the walls. If they closed their eyes, they could imagine they were in one giant kitchen.

On footpaths they found crusts and all sorts of nibbles. Vegetable scraps spilled from bins and collected in drains.

"Yippee!" yelled Meggsie. He dived from the gutter and rolled merrily in the litter.

"Shut up, will you!" snapped Magnus. "Or you'll ruin everything."

"There's food for all the family," said Meggsie. "And more, more than all of us would ever eat. I could get to like living here."

"Haven't you noticed there are no mice around?"

"All the more for us."

"But there are cats." Magnus felt a prickling down the back of his neck.

"They're very well fed," said Meggsie, and went on munching.

"Don't be too sure." Magnus gazed at Meggsie sitting there among the vegetables. "Would you mind getting up and helping me find somewhere safe to go?"

He dragged Meggsie out of the gutter and pushed him behind a drainpipe. "Take a proper look around."

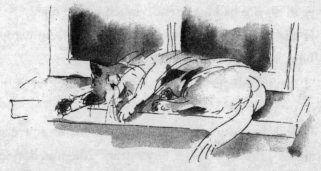

There were cats asleep in doorways, on car hoods, and on roofs and windowsills. Some preened and stretched and sniffed the air.

For a second, Magnus saw the face that had leered down at him in the pet shop, before the owner dragged it away. That cat had tapped and taunted Magnus with its paw. "They might look as if they're playing," he told Meggsie. "But they've got sharp teeth and claws. I know cats!"

He led Meggsie into a basement parking lot, where they might be safe when daylight came. They crouched behind a signboard that said PLEASE PAY AT THE DESK. Cats stalked past the window above their heads.

"Like I said," lectured Magnus. "Keep out of sight— or we'll both be goners. The can-clattering, slum-bum alleys are not for us."

Meggsie lay back, rubbed his stomach, and burped. Never in his life had he eaten so much in one night.

"I wish you'd keep quiet," said Magnus. "And stop laughing, will you!"

"I can't." Meggsie pointed at him. "Look at your belly, you're so fat!"

"Speak for yourself! You won't be able to squeeze through a grate if you get any fatter." Magnus hoped Miranda wasn't hungry. "Where do you think she is, Meggsie?"

"Who?"

"Miranda."

"Will you *stop* going on about Miranda!"

"I can't."

She didn't stop to think about food. The important thing was to reach the end of the bracken.

Fern fronds shut out the sun so at times she couldn't tell whether night had come. She had no idea how much farther she must travel. Perhaps she was going around in circles. But onward she pressed, blocking the eerie sounds and scary sights from her mind. Keep thinking of the stable, she told herself. Smell the straw, taste the oats . . . keep going.

Nearing the bottom of the gully, where the forest seemed thickest, she glimpsed light ahead. She pushed faster, farther, faster till at last she burst through the bracken into daylight.

She found herself in a dry creek bed, facing open country. On the other side of the valley, ponies grazed behind neat white fences. Farm buildings stood out like boxes that had been dropped from the air. A tin roof glinted in the late afternoon sun. Was that the stable?

She made her way up the hill to the shed. Its doors

hung open wide. She stood there and looked about her, dwarfed by giant machines and stacks of tools and tins and boxes. A sudden roar exploded behind the shed. Miranda jumped as a black sheepdog flashed around the corner. She heard the rush of its breath.

I'm gone! she thought. But she couldn't give up now. She rolled out of the dog's path and raced up a post with the dog barking at her tail. Keep climbing, she told herself—dogs can't climb.

She reached a crossbar and peered down. Magnus had shown her that humans weren't so big if you climbed up high. Dogs, too, were not so frightening when you looked down on them.

The dog leapt and squealed and ran in circles around the post.

It's only a yacker, she decided. She held on with all claws. It can't go on all night. But *I* will.

Next day Magnus and Meggsie

moved on to another district. Truly, the streets were paved with food.

But food wasn't enough. "We must find somewhere to call home," said Magnus. This one would be *his* home, and a place for all the family.

On the third evening, they came to a great building, lined with shops. ROYAL ARCADE said a sign over the entrance. People crowded in and out the doorway, and stood in groups, laughing and looking. Boots tapped on the tiled floor. On one side of the arcade bright lights flickered from the pinball parlor. Machines rattled.

Opposite, a flute played softly in a tea shop. Next door to the babywear boutique was a bookshop that smelled of old papers, then a toy shop and a jeweler and a cappuccino bar, frothing with teenagers.

In the center, a man was mending shoes.

"Wow!" said Meggsie. "Everything's here!" He skipped and kicked and turned handsprings.

"I told you not to show off!" said Magnus.

"I can't help it. I think I've got into the habit. No one took any notice of me before."

"And now we don't want them to," growled Magnus. "Keep walking!"

Farther into the arcade, a smell from another day

washed over him. He stopped and sniffed and scampered past the pet shop without turning his head.

"Don't you want to look inside?"

Magnus kept on going. "There's nobody I know there anymore."

He leaned back and gazed at the domed ceiling. It shone with gold paneling and painted bluebirds in gilt cages. This was, perhaps, some sort of palace. He couldn't help thinking how much Madeleine would like it. "But I want to find a place for all of us."

"I suppose you reckon it's too ritzy here," said Meggsie.

"But notice, no cats!" Magnus beckoned to him. "Let's take a look over there."

Alongside a china shop, a door opened to a narrow staircase. Wooden stairs led to a landing, and steps on to a second floor. The mice nosed around in the semi-darkness.

"I'll just slip out here," said Meggsie. He squeezed under a door and disappeared.

"Where are you?" yelled Magnus. Meggsie was a real worry at times. He thumped his foot on the floor and waited.

Blast Meggsie! If he wanted to be difficult, then

Magnus would go off looking on his own. He dropped behind a step and discovered a boarded-up space at the base of the landing. An air vent, like a window, gave it the look of a doll's house. He squeezed through the vent and found himself in the smallest room he'd ever seen.

It was no bigger than a fruit box, but it might be what he was searching for. The boards were hard, like the bathroom, but clean and dry. Nobody had been here before. Magnus took a deep breath and fluffed into a contented ball.

When he looked up, he saw Meggsie's toothy grin through the bars of the vent.

"Wait till you see what I've found," said Magnus.

Meggsie flipped between the bars. "It's only a space under a staircase."

"Exactly. No good for anything but a family of mice. Our own private house!" He rattled the grate. "And our own security door. No cats can get us here. Do you think it'll do?"

"It's the best we've seen," said Meggsie. "I knew we'd find something."

"Yes, we did."

They sat side by side, with the arcade music a dull thud away. "Madeleine will like the music," said Magnus.

"Murgatroyd won't like the stairs."

"Mortimer will like the security entrance."

"Do you think Manuel likes fish-and-chips?"

And Miranda? "I would've liked to find Miranda something a bit more special," said Magnus.

Miranda didn't know how long she clung to the rail, listening to the dog yowling. She was scratched and weary, and weak from hunger.

This place could not be the stable. It smelled of oil and rust, with nothing comfortable about it.

From her perch she could see another building, enclosed by a fence and gates. *That* must surely be the stable.

The dog's cries grew weaker. It gave a few more half-hearted yaps and yawned. At last it lost interest and slunk away.

Miranda slid to the ground and scurried across the yard and under the fence. She knew before she entered that this was the right place. Magnus had described the smells perfectly. The stable was warm and fresh and welcoming.

Miranda sneaked under the door into a passage with

stalls along one side. A horse snorted and swished its tail, and let her pass. Another gazed over its gate and whinnied. These were friendly animals. They would not hurt her.

She scurried into an empty stall and sniffed about her. Food! Spilled oats lay in corners and under the straw bedding. It was weeks since she'd had such a feed. There was enough here for everyone.

Satisfied, she sank into the straw. Sweet, nutty smells hung about her. The horses munched gently, leaving her to rest. Above her head, she saw the loft bulging with hay. A wooden ladder leaned against the landing.

Upstairs was always better than downstairs, she knew. She climbed the ladder and slipped between the hay bales to the back of the loft. There, shielded even from the moonlight, she made herself a bed. The hay wrapped itself around her in a soft hug. While she nestled there, the horses nickered like neighbors, telling her everything would be all right.

Yes, this is the place, she said.

Eighteen

Magnus and Meggsie spent the day lulled into a contented sleep.

When evening came, it was time to head back to Whereabouts. Magnus hurried Meggsie through the arcade. "Don't stop till we reach the street."

They followed their noses to a bin on a shadowy strip of the pavement. Takeout food wrappings littered the path. They sniffed out greasy chips and half-eaten hot dogs. "I'll miss all this," said Meggsie, and burrowed farther inside a hamburger carton.

"You've got used to eating," said Magnus. "Like we nearly got used to being hungry." He sat back, knowing he'd had enough. Meggsie went on eating.

Magnus looked up and down the street, working out which way to go. "It *is* dark tonight. Hope we can find our way."

Feet chattered past them. Then suddenly, across the footpath under the post office steps, Magnus saw a mouse. Could it be? This was the first mouse he'd seen here in the city. As he stared, the mouse smiled at him.

Magnus smiled back. "Hey, Meggsie!" he called. "Come here!"

By the time Meggsie emerged from the hamburger bun, the mouse had gone.

"What's up?" asked Meggsie.

"Oh, nothing." Had he imagined they were not alone? "Let's get going."

They set off toward the station, choosing back streets away from pounding feet and fast cars.

"Are you sure this is the way to the station?" said Meggsie. "It's so black tonight."

Magnus didn't stop to worry about it. The stars were hidden by clouds, and he didn't recognize any fruit stalls or trash bins. But he felt sure he would find the station. "Follow me!" he said, and sauntered ahead.

When Meggsie caught up with him, Magnus slung his tail around Meggsie's ribs. "Guess what, Meggsie," he said. "Someone I don't know smiled at me tonight."

Together they romped along the alleys. The city lights were still shining, when in the distance they heard the day's first train roll away from the station.

They'd done what they came here to do. Soon they'd all be city mice, and no one would be hungry again. In his head, Magnus went over what he'd tell Miranda. He couldn't wait to see her face.

A street-sweeping van brushed past and sent them scurrying out of the gutter onto the footpath. The smell of garbage wafted past them.

"Just one last meal before we leave?" asked Meggsie. He eyed a garbage can on the corner of the street.

"I don't suppose it would do any harm," said Magnus. He rested against a wall while Meggsie climbed up the side to investigate the can.

Magnus didn't see the cat streak across the footpath and pounce.

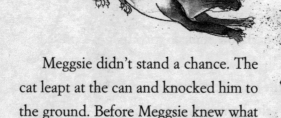

Meggsie didn't stand a chance. The cat leapt at the can and knocked him to the ground. Before Meggsie knew what had hit him, the cat grabbed him in both paws and sank its teeth into his neck.

"No!" shouted Magnus. "No, no! Let go!" Meggsie's gargling shriek hit him, as if he too had been struck down. Each time the cat shook Meggsie, the cries grew weaker. It didn't sound like Meggsie at all.

One last meal. A sickly taste surged into Magnus's throat. It left his mouth dry and furry. He'd watched Martha die. Not Meggsie, too.

It was useless standing there, just watching. Without thinking, Magnus rushed at the cat and bit its ear.

With Meggsie still in its jaws, the cat swiped at Magnus with its paw. Magnus held on and kept on biting. The cat snarled and shook its head, dropping Meggsie to the ground. It turned, squealing, as Magnus let go of its ear. He watched the cat slink away.

Passersby heard the cry and saw only a bloodied mouse, lying beside a trash can.

Magnus darted off and hid in a plot of soil, covered by fallen leaves.

"Ooh!" A young woman stopped to look at Meggsie squirming on the footpath.

"It's only a mouse," said a man with her. "Come on, we'll be late."

Others came to look and moved on.

"It's far gone," said an old man.

"Forget it," said another.

A child pulled her father by the hand. "Can't you do something?"

"Yes," said the man. "We can put it out of its misery."

"Finish it off," said a boy. "But we need a spade."

Meggsie lay on his back, struggling to get to his feet. His tongue hung from his mouth. Blood smeared his chest, staining his coat a dirty red.

Magnus shivered under the leaves. Was this to be the end of their journey?

"A boot will do," said the man.

"Stamp on it!" said the boy.

The man raised his foot.

Magnus dashed from behind the bin and nipped his ankle.

The man fell back on his heel. "What the . . . !"

Magnus had disappeared.

"It was another crazy mouse!" said the boy.

" . . . saving its friend," said the girl.

"Let the wretched thing rot, then," said the man, and walked away. "I've had enough!"

The three left Meggsie there, alone. Nobody else worried about him.

Magnus edged from his hiding place. "Meggsie, it's me."

Meggsie opened his eyes.

"Can you move?"

Meggsie shuffled onto his side. "Don't worry . . . about me."

"Don't be stupid! I'm not leaving you here!"

Meggsie took a short breath, and then another. "Sorry, Magnus . . . sorry."

"Shh, Meggsie. Can you try, please try, to get to that sand over there."

It was only a cornstalk's distance to the safety of the plants, yet to Meggsie it seemed a world away.

He raised his head and gazed at Magnus. "I'll try."

Magnus laid his paws under Meggsie's body and eased him to his feet. "Just crawl. Come . . . you can rest there."

Meggsie coughed, and his body trembled. But he took a small step, and another, fumbling forward on his stomach, not lifting his body from the ground. A thin red trail followed him.

"See," said Magnus, and his comforting voice hid the

pain that he felt too. "Nearly there!" He stood in the plot and pulled Meggsie under the shelter of the leaves.

Meggsie sprawled in the sand and closed his eyes.

"Don't!" cried Magnus. Don't die, he wanted to say. "Don't go to sleep. You must just rest, get back some

strength." He licked the blood from Meggsie's coat. "You'll be all right—I know you!"

Meggsie opened one eye. "Tell me . . . tell me why . . . why am I always such a nuisance?"

"Shh, Meggsie, you're my friend."

Nineteen

Daylight had come, and it was a gray day. Magnus tried to throw off the gloom that belonged to the sky and had now become a part of him. He peeped through the leaves at the busy footpath.

Beside the wall, through the rush of moving feet, he saw the smile from the night before. He looked again, and it was still there.

"Who *are* you?" he called. "Can you come over?"

There was no answer, but this time the smile didn't disappear. It grew bigger, as the mouse wove between feet toward him. Then it turned and ran back to its hiding place.

"Come here!" called Magnus. "Don't go away!"

Again, the mouse crept toward them, and stopped, then came again.

"Don't be afraid," said Magnus.

"I'm not," said the mouse.

"Then get in here." Magnus made room in the sand for the visitor. "Who are you?"

"I'm Maxie, and I've been watching. Let me help." He began to clean Meggsie's wound. "Rotten cats! Why do they want to kill us? There now, it isn't as bad as it looked."

"Where were you heading?" asked Magnus.

"Home. What about you?"

"Home."

"Then we're going to the same place."

Magnus thought for a moment. "I think . . . that there are many different places, and they're all called home. As a matter of fact, we're changing ours. Where's yours, anyway?"

"I . . . er . . . that's the trouble. We came to the city to find food, and I've been here now, I don't know how many sleeps."

"You'd know your way around, then. Could you tell us the quickest way to the station—if I can get Meggsie there."

Maxie pointed to the church spire. "See that tower? Well, you don't go there." He waved toward a patch of green. "See that park . . . you don't go there. And over there's the stadium ... you don't go there, either."

"Where *do* we go?"

"I'm telling you."

"No, you're not," burbled Meggsie. His eyes were shut, but he was listening.

"Shh, Meggsie, leave this to me."

"I'm making sure we don't get lost," said Maxie.

"We?"

Maxie hung his head. "Sorry, I mean ... you don't suppose ..."

"Go on," said Magnus.

"You don't suppose I could come with you?"

Magnus sighed. "Why didn't you ask?"

"He *is* asking," said Meggsie.

"Shut up, Meggsie!"

"Shut up yourself!" snapped Meggsie.

Magnus nuzzled Meggsie's neck, and chuckled. "Oh, Meggsie, you're going to be all right."

"Sorry to interrupt," said Maxie. "But like I said, can I come too?"

"I thought you lived in the city," said Magnus.

Maxie shuffled in the sand. "Not exactly. I'm on my own, see. The others went off without me."

"They left you here, on your own?"

"The trouble is, I'm a ditherer."

"What does a ditherer do?"

Meggsie groaned. "He gets left behind."

"I can't seem to say what I mean, or do what I want to do. We came to the city for the day, and I didn't want to come, and then I didn't want to go home, and when I did I couldn't find the way. I've been following you, for a while."

"Would you two stop talking," said Meggsie. "Can't a fellow get any sleep?"

"Stay with us," said Magnus.

It was good to rest and recover under the leaves. A deepening dark closed on the city as if shutters had come down on the day. Magnus peeped from their shelter and thought that evening had come.

Maxie pulled him back. "It's early yet." He sniffed. "There's something strange in the air today."

"I hope not," said Magnus. "We've had enough for one day."

Twenty

Magnus kept watch over Meggsie and listened to Maxie's snores. While he counted the hours, the city hummed around him, and he knew Maxie was right. There *was* something different in the air today. Rumblings louder than trucks rolled behind the thrum and bustle he'd come to know.

"Wake up," he said, and shook Maxie. "Let's get going."

Together they lifted Meggsie to his feet. "Can you stand?" asked Magnus.

"I can stand," said Meggsie. He flinched. "And I can walk."

Maxie put a paw under his chest to support him. Magnus propped up the other side. "Slowly . . . we'll make it."

"This way," said Maxie.

"Not that way?"

Maxie tried not to grin. "I said this way, didn't I?"

They half-carried Meggsie along the gutters. When he stumbled, they heaved him back on his feet. When he gasped with pain, they paused to rest.

At times, Magnus thought they'd never make it. "Keep going," he said to himself. "Don't think how much farther, just keep going."

Small drops of blood seeped through Meggsie's coat. His mouth hung open as he struggled for breath. He shook the others away. "Go on . . . leave me here."

"Come on, not far to go, nearly there." Magnus lifted him gently. One paw after another, they edged ahead, each step draining the life from their legs.

"Don't think," mumbled Magnus. "Just keep walking."

Then Maxie stopped. "Look now, look up! It's the station."

In the shelter of a magazine stand, they watched the trains come and go, while Magnus looked for Platform 8. "That's where it came in."

"So the other side's where it goes out, eh?" said Maxie.

"Sounds mad enough to be right. Okay, then?"

They dragged Meggsie down the steps, along a tunnel, and up more steps to Platform 9. When the train pulled into the station, they jumped into a car and hauled Meggsie through the open door. He collapsed on the floor as the doors clicked shut.

"Meggsie!" Magnus whispered in his ear. "You can't lie here. Try, please try..."

Meggsie lifted his head and flopped back on the floor.

"Don't give up now," said Magnus. He and Maxie pushed and pulled Meggsie to safety under the nearest seat. They left behind a smudged red trail.

Only now did Magnus realize how tired he was. "Go to sleep, Meggsie," he said, and his voice faded into nothing.

When he opened his eyes, Maxie was awake and listening.

"What's that flashing and banging?" said Magnus. "What's happening?"

"I think it might be rain."

"Rain? I've never seen that."

"I did once see rain, but never like this. A river is falling from the sky."

"I knew something was going to happen," said Magnus. "The sun didn't shine today. Now, how do we get through this river?"

"Perhaps it will stop and go back up again."

Meggsie opened his eyes. "What's going on?"

"The sky's collapsed," said Magnus. "And there's a lot of water."

Meggsie nodded and didn't seem to understand.

"I don't like to tell you, but we have to get out soon," said Magnus.

"I can't swim," said Maxie. "Do you think we could stay on here, and see what happens?"

"No, we can't," said Magnus. "Is that what ditherers do?"

Maxie didn't answer. "Come on, then, Meggsie," he said. "We're off again."

When the train stopped at Wyetown, they splashed into a torrent of water. The sky must be angry, thought Magnus. It hurled down rain like missiles, battering them to the ground and soaking them to their skin.

They sloshed through puddles, searching for the road. They could hardly see where it began. Water gurgled in the gutters. They plunged into potholes overflowing with mud.

Meggsie stumbled and sank into the ruts. Magnus and Maxie lifted him and carried him on, half-swimming through the flood. We'll all be washed away, thought Magnus. This is surely the end of us.

Debris floated past, flushed out of drains and ditches. Paper, plastic, bits of cardboard, and ice-cream sticks buffeted them and knocked them off balance.

Maxie reached out and grabbed a small food carton as it swashed past. "Hold this!" he yelled at Magnus. "Take it over there!"

Together they dragged the carton to higher ground. "A boat," said Magnus. "Why didn't *I* think of that?"

They hauled Meggsie into the carton and launched it onto the roadway. The two mice pushed as it slid across the mud. When the boat foundered, they eased it ahead.

"This has saved us," said Magnus. "We'd never have made it without a boat."

"It won't last much longer," warned Maxie. "The bottom's beginning to cave in."

Magnus wanted to say it was because Meggsie had eaten too much, but it didn't seem the right time for jokes.

"It'll last," he said. "We're into the homestretch now."

He knew it, without looking. The place sounded like home. Gone was the drone of traffic that never stopped. Hushed were the tapping feet, the clattering voices. Here, the air sang a silent song. He wanted to sing himself, but they were not quite home yet.

Ahead, a light shone in the old boy's house. They staggered on. Their heads ached, and the cold seeped through their wet coats. But they could tell the rain was stopping.

Dawn dripped from the eucalyptus, revealing fields like a wide brown river stretching as far as they could see. Morning squelched under their feet. A truck swished past and spattered them with mud. They looked at one another, and all but their eyes were the color of the country.

"We all look the same!" said Magnus.

The others didn't seem to care.

"How much farther?" asked Maxie.

"Nearly there. How are you going, Meggsie?"

"I'll make it," he wheezed. "But the bottom's fallen out of the boat."

Finally they were at the gate of Whereabouts. Magnus couldn't believe they'd come this far. He would never have done it without Maxie. "It's strange," he said, "that you came along just when we needed you."

They stumbled up the driveway, supporting each other like soldiers limping home from battle. The house stood silent, surrounded in mud.

"Through there," said Magnus, and pushed Maxie under the wall outside the bathroom. The pipe was wet and slippery. He eased Meggsie along, toward the gap in the floor.

"Now!" He knew he was shouting. He couldn't control the excitement in his voice. Only another tail's length, and he'd be there!

Twenty-one

They've left us!" said Meggsie. "Nobody's here."

The bathroom was deserted. A smell of damp saturated the small quarters. Water lapped over the boards and covered the mice's feet.

"Gone!" said Magnus.

"Was *this* home?" Maxie peered at the sludge on the walls.

Magnus flopped in the slush, too disappointed to answer. "So what do we do now?"

"We find them," said Meggsie. "I'm not finished yet."

"Good," said Magnus, ashamed of himself.

He and Maxie helped Meggsie back along the pipe into the garden.

"Yes! Yes!" A voice shouted when they appeared. "It's them!"

"Manuel!" said Magnus. "Where did you spring from?"

"The toolshed," said Manuel. "They made me the

g-g-guard—keeping watch for you. We got flooded out of the b-bathroom."

"The toolshed?" Magnus was glad they wouldn't be there for long.

"It's t-terrible. All rust and r-rubble and no food anywhere." He bounced in excitement as he led them across the yard. All the time, he gazed at Magnus. "You're r-really back!"

They squeezed through a crack into the gloom of the toolshed. "Here they are!" cried Manuel. "I've found them!"

"Ach," said Mortimer. "Come up."

"They're on the w-workbench," explained Manuel.

Magnus heard a faint clink and patter, and Miranda stood in front of them. The smile vanished from her face.

She's still angry with me, thought Magnus. She doesn't want to see me.

"We're back," he said flatly.

Miranda was so shocked, she could hardly speak. "Magnus, what happened?"

"It's the rain. And Meggsie's hurt."

"Come up!" called Mortimer.

"Could you come down?" asked Magnus.

The mice climbed to the ground, cheering and laughing when they saw the bedraggled three standing, dripping, at the door.

"And who's this?" asked Mortimer.

"Three drowned r—" said Madeleine. Then she gasped. "Meggsie! What's wrong? You *are* hurt!"

Meggsie sank to the ground. The mice gathered around, nosing him, stroking him, fussing over his wounds.

Magnus didn't know what to tell them first.

"This is Maxie," he said. "We've had such a time getting back. And he helped us."

"Been in the wars, eh?" said Murgatroyd. "You all need a wash and a good rest."

"A wash! We've been nearly washed away! But please, will you look after Meggsie?"

The mice licked their paws and rubbed the mud from

the travelers' coats. "Tch, tch," muttered Murgatroyd as he parted the hair on Meggsie's shoulders. "You've been in a real fight."

"It was a cat," said Magnus. "And Maxie helped us. Would it be all right, do you think, if he stays?"

"Ach, why not?" said Mortimer. "He's a mouse, isn't he?"

It was easy when you were a real mouse, thought Magnus.

"Is Maxie one of your relatives?" asked Madeleine as she groomed Magnus's coat.

"Just someone we met in the city," said Magnus. "He was lost."

"I saw him," said Maxie. "Because he was white, I noticed him—and I followed them. Magnus gave that cat a real fright!"

Madeleine went on scrubbing and brushing. "There, you're shiny white again!"

"Magnus the White!" shouted Manuel.

Magnus felt his ears go pink.

Murgatroyd sat hunched up and nodded slowly. "It's a miracle you got home."

Miranda smiled at Magnus. "Tell us what else happened in the city."

"I found us a palace," he said softly.

"I knew you would!" cried Madeleine.

Murgatroyd shuffled and cleared his throat. "And Miranda has found us a stable!"

"A stable? How? Where did you go?"

Miranda's eyes glistened. "Remember what you told me . . ."

A stable! thought Magnus. "Yes, I remember."

"It's just like you said." She nestled closer to him. "It's more friendly, and comfy, I think, than anywhere. There's food, too," she said, watching for a sign that he was pleased.

He bent and nibbled her ear.

The warmth on her face was like the glow in his mother's eyes when she'd spoken of the stable.

"So . . . so what do you say?" asked Miranda.

He blinked, as if he'd been dreaming. Oh, brave and amazing, multimagnificent mouse! He smiled at her. "It'll be perfect."

"Better than the city, I think," said Meggsie. "Not so many cats!"

Maxie agreed. "The city's a great place for a holiday, but you wouldn't want to live there."

"So when are we m-moving?" asked Manuel.

"As soon as Meggsie's better," said Mortimer. "And now, everybody upstairs!"

The mice clambered up to the workbench.

"I don't think I can," said Meggsie.

"I'll stay down here with Meggsie," said Magnus. He knew what it was like to sleep downstairs, alone.

Twenty-two

Slowly the wounds began to mend. Aching limbs moved freely again, and Meggsie's cuts healed over.

The country, too, was recovering from the flood. Blue skies brought a fresh outlook. The soggy ground dried out, and the mice ran across the paddocks at night without sinking in mud.

Food was still hard to find. It would be some time before the grass sprouted and seeded again. The mice were impatient to leave for their new home.

"How did you find it?" Magnus asked Miranda. "How did you get through the bracken?"

"I *had* to get through it," she said. "It was scary at times, but I kept thinking of what you'd told me . . . and I knew I'd make it."

The warmth inside him swelled until his feelings spilled over. He nibbled her cheek. "I . . . I don't know what I'd have done . . . if you hadn't come back."

She fluffed herself up and nestled beside him. "Me too," she whispered.

Maxie wandered past and winked at Madeleine. "I *knew* he was in a hurry to get home."

"One is thankful," said Madeleine, "that he came to us in the first place." She sidled toward Maxie. "And that he brought you."

"Yeah, mate!" Meggsie gave Maxie a playful nip on the neck. He jigged on one leg and then the other to show he was almost fit again.

"Let's g-get going!" said Manuel.

"Right," said Mortimer, and called the mice together for the last time in the toolshed. "The day has come for us to leave this place. When the sun goes down this evening, we'll set out for our new home."

At the end of the day, the mice straggled from the shed and across the yard. For a moment, Magnus stopped for a last look at the house to which the boy had brought him. There was the window to the boy's room. Inside, he supposed, stood an empty cage that looked like a castle.

Miranda called back to Magnus. "Hey, Mousie, aren't you coming!"

He scurried to join her.

In the paling light, the boy stood alone on the verandah and watched the mice run past the house. He stayed till they crossed the paddock, over the first green shoots of autumn, and disappeared into the bracken.

Then he turned and went inside.

Turn the page for a preview of the next
Magnus Maybe adventure

Missing Mem

by ERROL BROOME
pictures by ANN JAMES

Magnus Mem

Available soon from Simon & Schuster

The whole world smelled good that day.

Magnus shuffled closer to Miranda and settled into the warm hay, waiting for dusk.

"Comfy, eh?" he whispered.

"Everything's fine," she said.

Yes, he thought, everything was fine. They couldn't have a cosier home than their snuggery, here in the stable loft. The horses below were almost like friends to them.

Then why did his whiskers prickle like this?

His three young ones were beginning to stir, and he could feel Mem's eyes watching him. Something about her troubled him. He stretched his neck and smiled at her—Mem, the only one who'd turned out white like him. She sat apart from her brother and sister as they nudged one another awake.

Manfred wagged his too-long whiskers and nipped Millie's ear.

She squealed and leaped in the air and began to chase him around the loft.

Magnus edged through the hay and huddled beside Mem. "All right there, eh?"

She turned away, and even in the shadows he could see the blush on her ears.

"Come on, you can tell me."

She looked up at him, and spoke softly. "Why am I so different?"

"But you're not."

Her eyes were like liquid rubies. She blinked at him. "You know I am."

"You're the same as me. What's wrong with that?"

"Oh, I *want* to be like you."

He touched her gently on her pink nose. "There'll be times, Mem, when it's hard. I know. But here we're family. You're the same as everyone else."

Manfred and Millie flicked hay in her eyes as they scurried past. Mem snuffled a small sigh. "I miss Madeleine. She was different from other aunts. Why did she have to go?"

"She and Maxie needed to make a home of their own.'

"I thought she liked me."

"Everybody likes you," said Magnus.

Mem's voice wavered, as if she wasn't sure. "If . . . if I could just find someone like me . . . a friend of my own."

"But Mem, you'll have lots of friends," said Magnus, and in that moment he promised himself that he would always help her. "I *know* you will."

She snuggled against him. "I won't be worworried when you're here."

"*Worried*," he said with a toothy snort. He gazed at his daughter's small, sweet face and the gleaming white of her coat.

"Didn't you notice, Mem, the way Madeleine used to look at you? She'd have given anything to be white, like us."

Her jewelled eyes opened wide. "Truly?"

"Truly. Be proud, Mem, and you'll shine like a star."

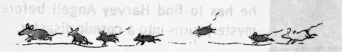

ary's
and
But
ry—

vers
his
ping
rvey
ald

in
ae
ke
nd
his

Aladdin Paperbacks • Simon & Schuster Children's Publishing Division
www.SimonSaysKids.com